the last stream

CM CAMPBELL

To my fiancé. Thank you for… well, obvious reasons. 🤭
To my pen sisters. Y'all sat through every crashout, meltdown, and "what if I just burned this whole book?" moment. Saints, truly.
To my beta and ARC readers. You willingly signed up to pick through my chaos and somehow made it better. I owe you snacks.
And to Tiffany, my very first Patreon supporter. You're basically this book's godparent.
Thanks for rocking with me. You're all stuck with me now.

SIX YEARS apart didn't change the way he looks at me.

Or the way I try not to look back.

We were supposed to be friends. Safe.

But the night he came home, he stepped into my world like he'd never left—and took something I didn't even know I'd been holding back.

Now the rules we lived by are gone, and the line between us isn't just blurred.

It's gone.

And I'm not sure I want it back.

trigger warnings

A.K.A. THIS AIN'T YOUR SWEET, SLOW-BURN FRIENDS-TO-LOVERS

Oral fixation
Anal play and penetration
Sex toys
Praise kink
Light degradation
Possessive dominance that leaves zero room for doubt who
she belongs to
Orgasm control and denial
Voyeurism
Hair pulling, chin-gripping, and manhandling
Years of pent-up tension
Proceed if you want a man who waited six years, came
home for one woman, and intends to ruin her for anyone
else.

This is for the girls who believe in second chances and third orgasms.

one

BILLS & BOOK DREAMS

THE HUM of my box fan blended with the rip of packing tape as I sealed another order shut. Coffee sat to my right, sweet with cream and heavy on cinnamon, the steam curling up in lazy spirals. My living room table was a battlefield of bubble wrap, padded mailers, and books stacked like bricks in a dream I was still building.

I reached for the next one in the pile, sliding *My Choice Is You* by Mel Dau into its padded envelope and smoothing the flap down. The stack waiting beside me was a line-up I was proud of—Lanette's *The Perfect Lap*, Netra Antionette's *Body Count*, Sun The Author's *His*, Brandon Massey's *Nana*, S.A. Crosby's *All The Sinners Bleed*, Jahquel J's *Capone*, Tay Mo'nane's *Inflamed In His Love*, and ML Bash's *Who Loves You Better*. Every one of them a Black author, every one of them a voice worth sending out into the world.

I slid each into its mailer, printed the labels, and lined them up like soldiers ready for deployment. These packages weren't just sales. They were seeds. The online shop had been my way of testing the ground before planting the whole garden.

Against the far wall, my vision board leaned where I could see it. In the center, cut in bold black vinyl letters, was the name that lived in my chest: *Rooted Words*. Around it were clippings of cozy reading nooks, dark wooden shelves, warm lighting that looked like it could hold stories and secrets. Little sticky notes with ideas—monthly book clubs, author signings, a kids' corner full of Black fairy tales—curved at the edges from how many times I'd moved them around.

One day, those shelves wouldn't be pictures. I could see it so clearly, it almost hurt. The bell above the door, the smell of fresh paper and spiced tea, the steady hum of voices finding themselves in books where they existed. That was the dream.

But dreams didn't pay Mama's light bill.

I glanced at the paper tucked halfway under my laptop. The total at the bottom had a circle around it, my handwriting pressing the numbers deep into the page. Mama's prescriptions were already handled for the month, but the electric bill had to be next. My savings account for *Rooted Words* had been sitting at the same number for three weeks now.

That's why I worked like this—morning coffee, cardboard dust on my fingertips, late nights staring into a ring light. That's why Siren existed. She wasn't a guilty pleasure. She was the one who kept the lights on. How Mama's medicine cabinet stayed full. How the dream I was holding didn't shrivel up from lack of water.

The fan hummed louder as the sun shifted higher, sending warm stripes of light across the floor. I taped the last package and slid it into my tote. The weight of it pulled on my shoulder as I headed out the door, heat wrapping around me before I even locked it.

The walk to the post office was short, but in Georgia

summer, it always felt longer. My shirt clung to my back by the time I pushed through the glass doors and stepped into the cool blast of AC.

"What you shipping today, baby girl?" Ms. Sheila asked from behind the counter, the same way she always did. She had that smile that made you want to tell her your whole life story.

"Books," I said, sliding the tote up onto the counter.

She raised a brow like she already knew. "You stay busy."

"Trying to," I said, and passed her the first stack.

She scanned the labels, lips curving into a knowing smirk. "Keep at it. The world needs more of this."

I smiled, not trusting myself to say more. Compliments like that made the dream feel too close, and I couldn't afford to get lost in it here.

When I stepped back outside, the heat wrapped around me again, thick as honey. I walked home slowly, letting my mind drift between the packages I'd just sent and the night ahead. Siren's audience didn't wait, and bills didn't either.

Inside, I dropped my keys into the dish on the counter, set the tote down, and let the quiet settle. This was the part of the day where I usually tried to rest for an hour or two, but my brain was already ticking through what I needed for the stream. The camera was charged. The ring light was ready. Outfits clean and waiting.

In the other room, the vision board leaned against the wall, the words *Rooted Words* catching the late-afternoon sun. I looked at it once more before heading to my bedroom.

If I wanted that sign to hang above a real door, I had to keep working. Keep selling. Keep building.

My phone buzzed before I even had the packages set down on the counter. Mama's name lit up, followed by a photo of her grocery list. Bread. Eggs. Milk. Her favorite tea. Little stars next to the brands she didn't compromise on, in the same way she used to mark my school supply lists when I was little.

"When you get a chance" in Mama's language meant "today if possible."

I slid my shoes back on, grabbed my wallet, and stepped back into the heat. Georgia summer had a way of sticking to you, wrapping around your skin like you owed it something. The store was just a few blocks away, but even that short walk was enough to have sweat slicking the back of my neck.

My feet moved on autopilot, but my mind was running numbers. The bills were handled. Mama's prescriptions were already covered for the month. Rent was paid. The credit cards were at zero for the first time in years. That last part still felt new.

A couple of years ago, I wouldn't have been able to say that. Back then, the debt felt like quicksand—every step forward just pulled me down deeper. That's why Siren was born. Not because anyone asked questions. Not because anyone knew. Siren was my secret, and I kept her that way.

At first, it was survival. Learn the angles, get the lighting right, play the part. Siren was my creation—a voice, a look, a rhythm I could slip into like silk. She was for the camera, for the tips, for paying off balances I didn't want to pass down to anybody else.

Now? Siren was the investment plan. She funded the dream—Rooted Words. The building I could see clear as day in my head. Dark wood shelves, a bell above the door, stacks of books by Black authors in every genre you could think of. The kind of store I wished existed when I was a girl.

The sliding doors to the grocery store whooshed open,

cool air washing over me. I grabbed Mama's tea first—habit. My mind wandered as I moved through the aisles, filling the basket with her list and a couple of things she hadn't asked for but always liked.

And like it always did when I wasn't careful, my mind drifted to Kairoh.

Two months. That was all that stood between us and the day he'd walk out free. Six years of phone calls, letters, and visits through glass had a way of burning someone into your life. Him sending money despite me telling him not to. His voice had been my constant, the one steady thing when everything else was shifting. The last time he'd called, he said, *When I get out, we're catching up.* Not a suggestion. A promise.

At checkout, the cashier smiled. "Hot one today."

"Feels hotter than yesterday," I said, swiping my card.

By the time I carried the bag up Mama's steps, my shirt was damp from the heat. She opened the door before I could knock.

"You didn't have to rush, Jay," she said, stepping aside.

"I was already out," I lied, setting the groceries on her counter.

She gave me a look like she didn't quite believe me, but didn't push. "Don't burn yourself out."

"I won't."

Back home, the quiet wrapped around me the second I shut the door. My tote was still by the counter, empty now but smelling faintly of paper and ink. Across the room, my vision board leaned where I'd left it. Rooted Words glinted in the fading afternoon light, surrounded by pictures of warm lighting, worn armchairs, and shelves packed full.

That's what all this was for. Not just keeping the lights on anymore, and not just staying afloat. I was building something, one stream, one package, one step at a time.

Tonight, Siren had work to do.

I'd just stepped into my bedroom, setting the grocery receipt on the dresser, when I pulled the blackout curtains closed. The late sun narrowed to thin strips across the champagne sheets. My ring light glowed to life in the corner, its warm halo already softening the edges of the room.

My phone buzzed in my back pocket. The name lit the screen, no need to check twice.

"Hey, Roh," I said, settling onto the bed with the phone to my ear.

"What you doin'?" His voice had that smooth, low weight to it that always seemed to settle right under my skin.

"About to start setting up for tonight," I said, glancing at the ring light. "Work's calling."

A quiet hum from his end, steady but unreadable. "Mm. How's your day been?"

"Busy. Orders packed and shipped, Mama's list handled. Now I'm here." I smiled a little. "And you? Same as yesterday?"

"Same as yesterday. Same as the day before. Look out for that money I sent you." His voice shifted—lighter, but carrying something underneath. "Two months and I'm out. Then we're not doin' this on a phone no more."

"Kairoh, I told you about sending me money, and I know. I'm ready for you to come home."

"And when that happens..." He paused just long enough for it to land. "Things change."

"Change how?"

"You'll see. Just know you won't be out here on your own anymore."

The words sat heavy in the air, not a threat, not a question—a fact.

"You sound real sure about that," I said.

"I been sure," he replied, low and even. "Six years, sure."

The timer warning beeped in the background, and he didn't rush his next words. "I'll call tomorrow."

"I'll be here," I told him.

"Yeah," he said, like he already knew.

The line clicked dead, leaving me alone in the warm light of the room. My hand drifted over the lace set still waiting on the chair. Siren had a show to run. But in the back of my mind, Roh's voice lingered like he'd spoken it right into my skin.

The coffee, the post office, the phone call with Roh — all of it faded under the slow, deliberate rhythm of my prep. Blackout curtains drawn. The ring light glows warm against the champagne sheets. The camera waited, an unblinking eye ready to catch every curve and glint of gold.

I opened the toy drawer and laid out the lineup on the bed like I was setting the table for a feast. The jeweled anal plug, polished and snug from earlier. The wireless vibrating egg, fully charged, sleek in my palm. The nipple clamps, gold bars shining, promising that sweet pinch. And the rose toy — soft, smooth silicone, pulsing with its own quiet heat from the charger. All of them ready. All of them mine to wield.

From the closet, I pulled the black lace set that always made the tips roll in. Sheer bra, cut to frame my breasts perfectly. Crotchless panties that hugged high on my hips and left nothing to the imagination. The lace robe was just for the opening act — Siren knew the value of a slow reveal. Last, I tied on the satin half-mask, the final step in locking Jaylah away and letting Siren loose.

The mirror didn't lie. Big curls spilling down my shoulders. Gloss catching the light on my lips. Nipples tight and already aching for attention. I took a slow breath and felt the shift inside — the shy girl gone, the sultry one in her place.

VIPs got the first taste. I sat on the edge of the bed, spreading my thighs just enough for the lace to part. Snapped one photo with the rose toy resting against my thigh. Another with my breasts cupped in my hands, gold bars gleaming between my fingers. Then a short video, my voice low and smoky: "Siren's warming up. You cumming or not?" Sent it off with a wink emoji.

The tips hit fast. Little chimes stacking into a melody. I smiled, set the phone on record, and angled it low so the frame caught my breasts perfectly. I clipped the nipple clamps on slowly, one by one, letting the camera catch the way my mouth parted at the sting. A soft hiss slipped past my lips, the kind that made men tip more. I let the chain sway once, teasing the gold between my fingers before ending the clip and sending it straight to my VIPs.

I adjusted the ring light, took my seat on the bed, and pressed **Go Live**.

The chat box popped instantly.

H-TownKing: Damn, you look good tonight.

Stacks4Siren: Skin glowing, baby.

ThirdWardTex: Missed this all week.

PeachFuzz281: Give me that smile.

"Evening, babies," I purred, letting the words drip slow and warm. "We're taking our time tonight. I've got something special for you."

I held the vibrating egg up for them to see, rolling it lazily over my palm. "First one to drop a thousand gets five minutes of control. Five minutes to make me feel exactly how you want me to."

Stacks4Siren: Mine.

The tip alert chimed, and I smiled slowly. "Looks like Stacks came to play." I dragged the egg between my lips, the slick silicone teasing over my clit before I slid it inside. The first pulse made my breath catch. I let my head tip back, hips shifting against the sheets.

H-TownKing: Talk to me, ma.

PeachFuzz281: Don't hold back.

"Mmm," I exhaled, letting the vibration hum through me. "You like watching me lose my breath?" I ran my hand over my stomach, down between my thighs, pressing the egg deeper in my pussy.

The chat filled with tip alerts, each one flashing their hunger across my screen. I reached for the rose toy, holding it close to the camera. "Two thousand, and I'll put this right where you want it." I brushed it lightly over my clit, my thighs twitching at the first pull of suction.

ThirdWardTex: Mine.

The bar filled in seconds. I placed the rose against my clit and moaned low, letting the sound curl into their ears. The suction and the egg together made heat pool low in my belly, and I rocked into it, giving them just enough to imagine the rest.

Stacks4Siren: Stay right there.

H-TownKing: That's it.

"You like seeing me work for it?" My voice stayed low, coaxing, pulling them in. "Every little sound I make… You bought it."

I pulled the rose away just before the edge, smirking at the flood of begging in the chat. "Patience, baby. We've got all night… if you can keep up."

I leaned back on my elbows, letting the chain between my nipples sway, feeling the weight and sting every time I moved. The camera caught it all — the arch of my back, the slow drag of my hand down my thigh, the gleam of the jeweled plug when I shifted just right.

PeachFuzz281: Show me more.

Stacks4Siren: Touch yourself for me.

I slid my fingers between my thighs, circling my clit just above where the rose had been, letting my breathing hitch in time with the egg's pulse. My eyes stayed on the lens, on them. "You want more, you know what to do."

The tips rolled in again, and I let the pace build — not for me, not yet, but for them. Siren never gave it all away too soon. This was control. This was making them beg.

I pressed the rose back to my clit, my lips parting around a low, drawn-out moan. The egg pulsed harder, my hips lifting, thighs clenching. I let the sound spill from me, not polished, not fake, just the truth of how good it felt to have them pay for every second.

"Keep going," I murmured, riding the vibration, letting them hear every hitch and gasp.

The screen blurred slightly as my eyes fluttered, but I didn't look away. Siren never broke eye contact.

Finally, I pulled both toys away, letting the tension snap like a bowstring. My chest rose and fell, my lips still wet and parted. "That's all you get… for now."

The egg's pulse had my thighs trembling. The jeweled plug filled me with a steady, delicious pressure, and my fingers circled my clit in slow, drawn-out swipes. I could feel the heat winding tighter and tighter, every movement feeding that edge I was chasing.

The comments were scrolling too fast to read them all.

Stacks4Siren: Just like that.

H-TownKing: Faster, baby.

PeachFuzz281: I'm so close watching you.

BigBankLou: Make it messy.

I was almost there.

two

FRESH OUT

THE MORNING AIR hit like something I had been starving for. Warm, heavy with summer heat, carrying the faint cut of fresh grass from somewhere beyond the lot. I stepped past the painted line and let the sun burn against my face, lungs stretching deep without a clock or a guard telling me when to move. The world didn't close in. It widened.

The CO shoved a battered manila envelope at me, eyes holding that slick smirk they give men walking out. "You'll be back," he said, like he could see my future.

"Not in this life," I told him, taking the envelope without breaking eye contact. Inside was my parole sheet, the dead watch they took six years ago, a neat stack of bills from my account, and the chain Jaylah gave me for my twenty-ninth birthday. I looped it around my neck and held it until the metal warmed, a reminder I wasn't stepping out broke or broken.

Malik's matte-black Charger idled at the curb, rumbling low. He leaned across the passenger seat with a grin only an older brother could wear. "Get in, little man."

"Still calling me that at thirty-five," I said, shutting the door.

"I thought you had two more months," he said as we pulled away.

"That's what I wanted y'all to think," I replied, watching the razor wire shrink in the mirror until it became a silver thread.

"You work a deal?"

"I worked on good behavior and kept my mouth shut," I said. No snitching. No shortcuts. Just clean time served, discipline, and making myself into someone worth stepping out as.

The city's noise came in slow—the hiss of a bus brake, a couple arguing half a block away, the hum of people moving. I let it all sink in. Every sound was proof I'd made it back.

Prison teaches survival. I wanted more. I lifted, I read, I learned the market from an old head named Carter who taught me stocks between carved table legs in the rec room. Started small—commissary money, a few dollars Jaylah put on my books. Watched it grow. By year four, I had more than a cushion. By year six, I had the kind of money that could build a future.

All of it had her name on it.

She kept me alive in there—calls, visits, letters. One night, I thought about her voice on the other side of the glass and promised myself she'd never need to wonder again if someone had her back. That night, I decided she wouldn't go without me providing something steady.

We rolled down the road with the city stretching open in front of us, the skyline jagged and clean in the distance. The air through the open window smelled like rain on brick. Six years since I'd felt it without a fence in the way.

"You still want to crash at my spot till you figure out where you're laying your head?" Malik asked.

"Yeah," I said. "Won't be long. Just need time to move some pieces."

He grunted. "And her?"

Her. Like he had to clarify who. Like we both didn't know I'd been living half my sentence on the sound of her voice through a phone that smelled like bleach.

"She doesn't know I'm out," I said.

His eyebrows rose. "You mean to tell me you're not calling her first?"

"No. She's gonna see me first."

The diner Malik stopped at hadn't changed. Still smelled like bacon grease and biscuits, still had the same cracked leather booths. I ordered like a man making up for lost years—salmon patties, grits, two eggs, toast, extra jelly. The first bite landed in my chest.

I kept quiet while Malik talked about the neighborhood, about who'd moved and who'd stayed. But my mind wasn't on the block. It was on Jaylah.

Six years ago, I put a man in the hospital for laying his hands on her. Didn't think. Didn't hesitate. When the cuffs clicked, I didn't regret it. By the time the gavel dropped, I'd already decided she wasn't gonna carry the weight for it. My name, my time, my story. She walked away with nothing on her but the clothes she had on.

Inside, I kept her voice alive like it was oxygen. Letters. Phone calls. Visits through glass. She made time stop when everything else was on hold. I used to press my hand against the glass and watch her line hers up, pretending skin could pass through a barrier that thick.

Malik watched me eat like he could read my thoughts. "You gonna tell her why you're out early?"

"Not on a call. She'll hear it from me when I'm standing in front of her."

"You think she's ready for that?"

"She's been ready. She just doesn't know it."

We left the diner and headed to his place. He tossed me a set of keys and pointed to the second bedroom. "You know the rules. You got a roof here till you don't need it. Don't be bringing heat to my door."

I unpacked what little I had. Fresh clothes. The paperwork they gave me. A chain I'd sent home for safekeeping. I texted her.

> You good?

She sent back,
Jaylah:

> Always. You?

I texted back.

> Better than yesterday.

She answered with a heart emoji. No speech. Just a promise.

Calls, texts, little messages—none of it could touch what I needed. A screen wasn't her. A line of words wasn't hers. Tomorrow, I'd have her standing in front of me.

Tomorrow, I'll walk into her space with money in my pocket, the truth in my mouth, and the lock turning under my hand. Tomorrow, she'll see me—not a voice, not a memory, but a man who paid for the right to be here in years and choices.

Tomorrow, I plan to learn every sound she makes with nothing between us but air.

I stretched out on the bed and stared at the ceiling, phone heavy on the nightstand beside me. No COs stomping in. No metal doors clanging shut. Just space. Too much of it. I picked up the phone and scrolled through old threads—her jokes, her check-ins, her little one-word answers when I asked if she was good.

Malik's spare room was too quiet for a man who'd been living in noise for six years. The TV played a game with the volume low, but I couldn't lock into it. I tried a shower. I tried food. I even folded the small stack of clothes Malik left for me, like lining fabric into neat corners could make my hands steady. None of it worked. Free air moved different in my lungs, and every breath dragged her with it.

Jaylah.

She had no idea the money I sent her didn't stop with commissary. First chance I got, I funneled more into her account. Birthday, holidays, days when I could hear the wear in her voice through the glass—I wired what I could. Then I grew it, and kept sending more. Quiet. Steady. She probably thought I had some cousin on the outside helping me. Truth was, I didn't want her touching empty pockets ever again.

My thumb hovered over her contact. Call her. Don't call her. What was I gonna say? *I'm out early. Surprise.* Nah. She deserved more than hearing it through static. She deserved me standing right there, so she could see I'd made it through everything I promised I would.

A knock at the door broke the thought. Malik leaned in, one shoulder on the frame. "You good?"

"I'm straight," I said, but he kept watching me like he didn't believe it.

"You going to see her," he said. Not a question.

I gave him a nod.

"You want me to roll?"

"No," I said. "This one's mine."

His eyes narrowed. "You got keys?"

I tapped my pocket. Metal pressed back through the fabric. The old house key. She'd told me once, on a visit, that she never changed the lock. Said she couldn't. Said it still felt like mine. I'd laughed at the time, told her she was being dramatic, then gone back to my cell and held onto that memory like it was oxygen. Now it was just a fact. A door I could open.

Malik studied my face a second longer, then stepped aside. "Text me when you're settled."

"I will."

Outside, the night sat thick and warm, summer heavy on the skin. Streetlights painted the block gold. Somewhere down the street, a dog barked twice and went quiet. A couple argued in the distance. A bus let off a sigh like a giant tired of holding its breath. I walked with my head up and my hands loose. The world looked both brand new and exactly the same. It smelled like rain had touched the pavement earlier and left.

My phone buzzed again in my pocket. I didn't check it. Didn't need to. Probably Malik making sure I wasn't about to lose my head, or maybe Jaylah tossing me one of those short, steady replies. Either way, it didn't matter. Tomorrow wasn't far enough.

I'd given six years to a choice I made in anger for her. I put a man in the hospital for laying hands on Jaylah, and I never apologized for it. Wouldn't. And I wasn't about to start now by letting time, distance, or another man tell me what she should or shouldn't have.

I reached the corner where the old bodega still held court. The owner's nephew, a teenager I used to pay to sweep my shopfront back in the day, spotted me and froze. Then he grinned like he'd just seen a folk tale walk out of the dark. "Roh?"

"Keep your head on straight," I said, passing him. He laughed, a little shaky, and I realized my face probably still carried that hard-time look. I didn't soften it. Not tonight.

The night held its breath when I turned onto her block.

Every step carried six years in it—letters folded until the creases wore thin, phone calls cut short by static, visits broken by glass thick enough to smother touch. All of it behind me now, and all of it leading here.

I killed the engine two doors down and sat with my hands loose on my thighs, breathing her name in silence. Jaylah.

The key felt heavier than it had any right to, warm from my pocket, biting against my palm like it wanted to remind me this wasn't a dream. She said she never changed the lock. I didn't blame her. That apartment was the only piece of us left when the system swallowed me whole.

Streetlights cast her building in soft gold. Lemon cleaner drifted down the hallway when I stepped inside. Same smell as years back, like nothing had moved while time swallowed me whole.

I paused outside her door, key pressed to my palm. The air buzzed in my chest, steady and sharp, every muscle tight with restraint. I'd played this moment in my head a thousand times from a metal cot—walking up, turning the lock, seeing her face tilt up at me. No script past that. Just her.

My knuckles brushed the wood once, twice. Habit. Then I slid the key in, turned it slowly, and stepped inside like I still had a claim.

Her living room was neat, warm. Vanilla oil. Paper and glue. A stack of padded mailers on the table. Small signs of the life she'd built without me.

The light in the bedroom spilled out across the floor. Music pulsed low, not the kind she used to dance to in my passenger seat, but heavier, slower, thick with bass. I moved toward it, drawn like I had no choice.

Then I stopped.

Her voice rolled out, low and smoky, words meant for somebody else. My pulse kicked hard as I reached the doorway and looked in.

And froze.

She was a vision in black lace and gold. Mask on. Curls spilling over bare shoulders. The jeweled plug caught the light when her hips shifted, flashing green like a signal. Her thighs were open for the camera propped in front of her bed, her hand toying with a rose toy she held just out of reach.

The air punched out of me. Six years of imagining her one way, and now this.

Shock hit first, sharp and cutting. Then heat rushed in after it, fast enough to leave me dizzy. Because no matter who was watching, no matter how she dressed it, I knew that body. I knew that voice. And I couldn't unsee the fact that she was giving it away to a room full of strangers.

I gripped the frame hard enough to bite wood into my palm.

She turned, like some instinct whispered she wasn't

alone. Her eyes landed on me behind the mask, shock flashing across her face before relief softened it. My name left her lips like a prayer.

"Roh."

My throat tightened and then smoothed. I stepped inside the light.

"Keep going," I said, voice steady. "Do not stop on my account."

I took another step, slow enough to make her wait for me, my eyes locked on the open slit in that black lace. No guessing, no peeling fabric aside — her pretty little pussy was right there, glistening, the jeweled plug catching the light just above it like a crown.

"Look at you," I said, my voice low, meant for her and no one else. "Sitting here letting them stare like you're for sale. You think they earned the right to see you like this?"

She shook her head, lips parting, but I didn't let her answer.

"No. They don't. That body?" I crouched in front of her, close enough that my breath brushed her inner thigh. "It's mine to touch. Mine to taste. Mine to make come apart."

Her hips twitched, the plug shifting with the motion, and I let my gaze drag up slowly, from her knees to her chest. "You're so damn perfect it's disrespectful. That mouth should only be saying my name. Those hips should only move for me."

Her hips twitched, the plug shifting with the motion, and I let my gaze linger there until she made a tiny, helpless sound.

"You're so fucking wet," I murmured. "Bet they think they can make you cum. Bet they're sitting there with their hands on their dicks, praying you'll give it to them." My eyes flicked up to hers. "You know better. You know the only one who can make this tight little thing sing is standing right in front of you."

Her breathing quickened, but she kept her thighs open like I told her, her hands clutching the bedding for balance.

I brushed my fingers over the swell of her tits, just enough to feel her shiver. "These? Mine. These luscious curves ? Mine. Every sound you make? That belongs to me too."

She swallowed hard. "Yes."

I smirked. "Say it again."

"Yes, Roh."

"Good girl."

I hooked a finger in the lace, dragging it lightly across her folds just to feel her tremble. "You've been keeping yourself ready for me, haven't you? All that oil you use, all that stretching with toys… just training for this moment."

Her eyes locked on mine, wide and unblinking. "I didn't think you—"

"I've thought about it every damn day," I said, my voice low but steady. "Six years of phone calls and visits, acting like I wasn't picturing you like this. Acting like I didn't know exactly what I wanted to do to you."

Her breath shook. "We were best friends…"

"We still are," I said, tracing her with the barest pressure, just enough to make her squirm. "I'm just not pretending that's all I want anymore."

Her lips parted, a sound catching in her throat, and I leaned closer, letting my mouth hover by her ear. "You're about to learn what it feels like when your best friend's been starving for you this long."

I pulled back enough to see her face, my thumb resting just above where she was throbbing for me. "And after tonight, you'll know exactly who you've been waiting for."

Her hips tilted, a silent plea, and I gave her what she'd

been chasing—pressing two fingers inside her, slow and deep, letting her take every inch. Her gasp hit me hard. I curled them just right, the way I'd imagined a hundred times, watching her lips part and her knees push wider without a single word from me.

I hooked one finger inside her, knuckle-deep with ease from how wet she was, and pressed my thumb to her clit, slow circles that made her whimper. "Such a good girl," I said, my tone dripping with ownership. "Pretty little pussy all swollen for me. Plug sitting right where I want it. I could spend all night making you gush in front of them."

Her thighs trembled, the muscles in her stomach tightening.

"Yeah, you're close already, aren't you?" I teased, curling my finger just right. "Gonna let me have the first squirt you've given in six years?"

She bit her lip and nodded, eyes locked on mine.

"That's my girl," I growled, increasing the pressure on her clit while my finger worked her spot, relentless. "When you cum, you make a mess. I want it dripping down your ass, soaking the bed, so they all know you only do this for me."

Her moans got higher, sharper, her hips rocking against my hand.

"Come on, baby," I coaxed, my voice low but demanding. "Show me this pretty little pussy knows who she belongs to."

She shattered with a cry, her thighs squeezing around my arm as a hot rush spilled over my hand and onto the sheets. I kept working her through it, watching every twitch and gasp until she sagged back, shaking.

When I met her gaze again, she looked wrecked and perfect. I smirked, brushing my thumb over her lower lip. "Now you know."

I straightened, glancing once at the camera still streaming to the men who thought they owned a piece of her. My hand found her chin, tilting her face up to me.

"This," I said, voice low and certain, "was the last stream. Turn off the stream and shower so we can talk, Mamas."

PUSHBACK

"THIS WAS THE LAST STREAM."

His voice was calm, but I saw the flicker in his jaw before he said it, like he'd been working through a dozen words and picked the sharpest one. The calm almost scared me more than if he'd shouted.

Roh didn't rush me. He reached over, closed my laptop, and the little red light on my camera blinked out. Just like that, the room went quiet except for my breathing and the faint bass still rolling from the playlist I'd queued before this all started.

On the bed, my phone kept lighting up, messages popping through so fast it looked like it might overheat. My instinct was to grab it — to manage, to control, to respond — but he caught my eye and gave a small shake of his head.

"Leave it," he said. His tone wasn't hard, but it was steady. "Whatever's blowing up on there can wait."

The way he said it made heat crawl up my skin, not from desire this time, but from awareness. Awareness that he had seen me in a way I had never meant for him to see me. Not like this. Not through a lens, with strangers sending money I'd never touch. I felt stripped down, exposed, and not just because the lace was still clinging to my body.

I surprised myself by listening. By letting the phone keep buzzing on the sheets while I sat there, trying to take him in.

Roh.

The boy I met when I was sixteen, and I thought I'd seen everything. The one who used to walk me home from school when the streetlights were coming on and my mom was working late. The one who saw me cry in the parking lot after my first heartbreak and didn't tell a soul. The one who would've thrown hands for me — and did.

The one who disappeared behind steel and concrete for six long years because of me.

Now he was here, taller, harder around the edges, but still him. And I didn't know what to do with the knot in my chest that felt like relief tangled with something much more dangerous.

He moved in close, not crowding me but close enough that the warmth from his body cut through the cooling sweat on my skin. "Let's get you cleaned up," he said.

"Roh—" My voice cracked on his name. I wanted to ask him a hundred things — why now, how, what this meant — but he didn't let me.

"All your questions get answers after your shower, Mamas." The way he said it, low and even, was the same way he used to talk me down when I was too mad to think straight.

I nodded because anything else felt too heavy.

He helped me up, one arm steady around my waist when my legs shook from more than just what we'd done. The lace rubbed against my skin, a reminder of the camera that had been watching us minutes ago. He eased it down with careful hands, nothing sexual in the motion now. Just care. He removed the plug as gently as if it were made of glass, his touch sure, practiced, but never rushing me.

By the time we reached the bathroom, I'd stopped trying to pretend I didn't need the way he stayed close.

The warm light flicked on, painting the tile in a soft glow. He reached past me to turn the shower handle. The pipes groaned like they hadn't been used all day, steam curling out to meet us.

"Sit," he said, nodding to the closed toilet lid. I obeyed, watching him kneel in front of me to take off the clamps. He worked slowly, thumbing over each spot until the sting faded, his eyes flicking up to check my face like he used to check my knees when I fell at sixteen.

"You good?"

"I don't know yet," I admitted.

He didn't push. Just gave a short nod. "Then we wait till you do."

The steam had already dampened the edges of my hair when he stood and offered me his hand. The callus across his palm scraped lightly against mine — a detail I shouldn't have noticed, but did.

He stayed by the door as I stepped under the spray. Heat poured over my shoulders, down my spine, and I braced my hands against the tile. The water wasn't just washing me — it was giving me space to breathe.

Still, my mind kept looping back. To the way his voice had sounded when he told me to keep going. To the look in his eyes, like he'd been holding that hunger for years. To the fact that this man, who'd been my friend for nearly twenty years, had never once told me he wanted me — and now I couldn't unknow it.

The sound of the water was loud enough to muffle everything else, but I could still feel him out there. Waiting.

When I was done, I turned the handle, and the spray faded to a drip. Steam clung to my skin as I stepped out. He was there, holding out a towel like it was the most natural thing in the world.

I wrapped it around myself, tucking the edge tight over my chest. The heat from the shower had my pulse in my ears, but it wasn't the only reason.

He leaned one shoulder against the doorframe, watching me without hurry. Not staring at my body — looking at me. Really looking.

"Feel better?" he asked.

"Physically? Yeah." My voice came out softer than I meant. "Everything else… I don't know."

His mouth curved, not quite a smile. "That's fine. We'll get there."

I stood there dripping, towel snug, heart thudding in a rhythm I didn't trust, knowing that once I stepped past him, nothing between us would ever be the same.

I shut my bedroom door behind me, leaning on it for just a second. His voice was still in my head, the echo of *We'll get there* settling somewhere between my ribs.

The steam from the shower had cooled on my skin. I crossed to my dresser, pulled out a pair of soft cotton shorts, and his old t-shirt from high school. Not the kind of thing that invited anything more. Just enough to feel like I wasn't standing here in a towel with him sitting in my living room.

The fabric whispered against my skin as I pulled it on. I caught my reflection in the mirror, hair damp and curling in ways I'd usually fix before streaming again. Lips still fuller than usual, eyes carrying something I didn't want to name.

Through the door, I could hear the faint creak of my couch when he shifted his weight. Not pacing. Not restless. Just *there*.

I padded into the living room with damp hair and clean clothes. The air in here felt different than the steam-filled bathroom, heavier, like it remembered what happened between us better than I wanted to.

I stayed standing even though my legs felt a little shaky. He had said his piece like it was the most natural thing in the world, like he had not just walked into my bedroom and snatched my soul with a camera rolling. My heart had not decided whether to sprint or stop completely.

Awareness that he had seen me in a way I had never meant for him to see me. Not like this. Not through a lens, with strangers sending money I'd never touch. Especially when he had been the one sliding deposits into my account all along, steady and quiet, never asking questions, never demanding thanks.

"You really gonna sit there like you didn't just do all that?" I asked, sharper than I meant.

One corner of his mouth lifted. "Do all what, Mamas?"

The way he said it made my stomach flip. That voice always slid under the skin first and asked questions later.

"You know exactly what," I shot back. "That wasn't… we've never. You've never even looked at me like that before."

He didn't deny it. He didn't even blink. "I've been looking," he said. "You just didn't see it."

The words dropped between us like something that had weight and edges. My pulse jumped, my mouth went dry. I opened my lips to speak, but he moved before I could find the words.

He stood from the couch and closed the space without

rushing, each step drawing the air tighter around us. When he stopped in front of me, we were close enough that I could see the darker ring circling his eyes. His hand lifted and skimmed the ends of my damp curls. Not tentative. Not rough. Confident, like he knew where his hands belonged.

"That sound you made when I had you shaking," he said, voice low enough to be private. "I've been replaying it since I walked out that room."

"Roh." I wanted it to be a warning. It came out like his name had been dipped in heat.

"You think I came in here for a stunt," he said, his thumb brushing the curve of my jaw. "I didn't. I came because I want you."

I scoffed because it was easier than letting that sink in. "You came because you wanted to prove a point."

He leaned in just enough for his breath to warm my cheek. "You want the point or you want the truth?"

"What's the difference?"

"The point is, I didn't like the idea of them having you." His gaze stayed steady on mine. "The truth is, I want you. Not just your body. You."

The words hit me in two places at once — in my chest and lower. I looked away because meeting his eyes while he said things like that felt like stepping too close to a ledge in high wind.

"You don't know me anymore," I said, quieter than I meant.

He didn't back off. "I knew you at sixteen, when you cried over a boy who didn't deserve you. I knew you at twenty-two, when you talked about getting free like it was something you could taste. I knew you every day you called me. And I know you right now."

"You sound real sure of yourself."

"I'm sure of you," he said, his voice steady. "And I'm sure of me when I'm with you."

I crossed my arms because I needed to keep my hands from doing something reckless, like grabbing his shirt. "You have an answer for everything."

"Only for what matters."

"And you get to decide what matters?"

"No," he said, calm as stone. "I'm telling you what matters to me. You decide if it matters to you."

It should have made me want to argue, but the truth in it caught me off guard. "You walked in here like you owned the place. You put your hands on me. You put your mouth on me. With a camera on."

"You could have told me to stop," he said quietly.

The heat that flashed through me had nothing to do with anger. "I know."

"You didn't."

There was no answer for that, and the silence between us stretched. He took one more step forward, erasing the last bit of space.

"That wasn't about showing off," he said. "That was me running out of patience. I've had years of it. When I saw you like that, it was gone."

My heart thudded hard. "So you came to prove you could make me fall apart?"

"I came to remind you of something you've always felt," he said. "And to tell you, I'm not letting a room full of strangers get more of you than I do."

The possessiveness in his tone should have raised my defenses, but instead, something in me loosened. "You're not my man."

"Not yet." It didn't sound like a threat. It sounded like certainty.

His hand caught the towel hanging around my neck,

giving it a gentle tug that brought me a fraction closer. "You smell like that oil you know that I love," he murmured. "I missed it."

My breath caught. "You need to stop talking like that."

"Why?"

"Because I'm trying to think and you're trying to make me feel."

He smiled slightly, like I'd just told him something he already knew. "You can do both."

I huffed out a quiet breath, not because I didn't believe him, but because I did. His certainty had always been dangerous to me.

"You've been gone a long time," I said finally. My voice wasn't sharp — more like I was testing how the words felt in the air. "I just… didn't expect this. Not tonight."

"I did." His eyes didn't waver. "I've been expecting it since before I saw you again."

The admission sent a small jolt through me. I didn't know if it was the kind you welcome or the kind you're supposed to resist, but it worked its way under my skin either way.

He was still close, close enough that the faint spice of his cologne wrapped around me. My pulse jumped when his fingers brushed the side of my neck, like he was making sure I was real.

"Why now?" I asked, quieter still. "You could've waited. Could've eased into it."

His mouth tilted like I'd just told a joke he understood too well. "I waited six years, Mamas. I'm not here to ease into anything. I'm here to take my shot while it's in front of me."

That landed in the pit of my stomach, warm and heavy. I swallowed, trying to keep my voice steady. "You're… different."

"Not different," he said. "Just done pretending I don't want you."

The directness stole my breath for a second. I shifted my weight, needing space but not taking it. "It's a lot to process."

He studied my face for a moment, then his hand slipped away from my neck, the heat of his palm lingering. "Then process. I'm not going anywhere."

Something eased in my chest at that. I hadn't even realized I'd been bracing for him to push harder.

"I don't know what this is yet," I admitted. "Or what I want it to be."

His gaze softened, though the confidence in it didn't fade. "That's fine. You figure it out. In the meantime, I'll be here, reminding you why it's worth wanting. I don't care who you've been for them. I want who you are when the lights go off."

Before I could find a response, he stepped in, closing the space so slowly it felt deliberate. His hand slid to the back of my neck, warm and sure, and then his mouth was on mine.

The kiss wasn't hurried. It wasn't tentative either. It was deep enough to make my knees feel unsteady, steady enough that I knew exactly what he was telling me without saying it. My fingers curled into the hem of his shirt before I realized they'd moved at all.

When he pulled back, my breath was uneven, my pulse too quick. He kept his hand where it was, his thumb brushing lightly against my skin.

"I'm leaving," he said, like it wasn't up for debate.

Something in me wanted to ask him to stay, but the words tangled in my throat. *Part of me wanted him to stay. Part of me was grateful he knew better.*

"Why?"

"Because you need time," he said simply. "And because when I come back, I want you knowing exactly what you want from me."

I held his gaze, the truth of it settling somewhere behind my ribs. My throat felt tight, but I still managed, "I'm glad you're home."

That got a real smile out of him — small, but it reached his eyes. "Me too, Mamas."

He let his hand fall from my neck, stepped back, and headed for the door. I followed him with my eyes until the soft click of the latch left the apartment quieter than it had been in years.

The warmth of his kiss still lingered, stubborn as a memory that refused to fade.

four

LINE IN THE SAND

MORNING BROKE SOFT BUT STEADY, sunlight slippin' through Malik's blinds and painting the room in weak stripes. I laid there a minute, eyes open, starin' at the dust caught in the glow. Mattress wasn't no prison issue, but it felt just as hard under me. Sleep ain't done a damn thing. My body rested, but my head ain't slowed once. Every thought circled back to her. Jaylah.

I sat up, draggin' a hand over my beard, coarse bristles scratchin' against my palm. She was still there behind my eyes. Not just her face—the fire in it, the softness she don't let most people see, the taste of her still sittin' on my tongue from the night before. Sweet and sharp at the same time, like somethin' forbidden I'd been waitin' too long to have. I thought finally touchin' her again, finally tastin' what I'd been starvin' for behind bars, would settle me. Instead it just woke up somethin' hungrier. I wanted more. Every piece of her, every sound, every look. Last night proved it wasn't no dream I built in a cell. It was real. And now that I'd had it, there wasn't no turnin' away.

But the other side cut deep. The way I first seen her, lit

40

up by that screen. I wasn't ready for that. Six years of prison noise, six years of sharpenin' myself for the day I walked free—and none of it braced me for seein' her givin' herself to strangers with fat wallets and empty hearts. She knew I was sendin' money. She took it, thanked me, told me it helped. But what I saw last night told me straight—it wasn't enough. Not when she was payin' rent, keepin' the lights on for her mama, coverin' bills while tryna stash for that bookstore she always swore would save her. I thought I was easin' the weight. Truth is, I was just coverin' the corners while she broke her back holdin' up the middle.

That stung worse than anything. Not anger at her, never that. Anger at myself, for the blind spot I let grow while I was locked up. I'd been in there thinkin' I was her lifeline, but she was out here bleedin' herself dry just to keep both they heads above water. And she never told me. She let me think the money was enough. Maybe she ain't want me carryin' more than I already was. Maybe she thought she was protectin' me from the truth. Either way, I hated knowin' she carried that alone.

I got up and paced the room, boards creakin' under my steps. That old street rhythm in me wouldn't let me sit still when somethin' needed fixin'. I'd spent six years learnin' patience, buildin' discipline, turnin' scraps into stacks. Played markets with pencil charts and whispers from men who lived off risk. Came out with more than I ever thought possible—and all of it, every cent, had her name on it. But last night showed me money wasn't just numbers. It was proof. Proof she ain't gotta strip herself down for people who don't see her like I do.

I leaned against the wall, jaw tight, fists flexin' open and closed. The thought of her smilin' at a camera for men who'd forget her the second they logged off lit somethin' dark in my chest. Not jealousy. Possession. Protection.

I'd bled for her before, put a man in the hospital for layin' hands on her. I'd do it again, no blink. But this fight was different. This wasn't fists. This was about makin' sure she never had to look at a camera and pretend again. Makin' sure she could finally breathe, finally rest, finally live like the dreams she used to whisper in my ear meant somethin'.

I remembered her laugh, the way it slipped out even when she tried holdin' it back. The way her mouth tasted under mine, soft and bold at once. The way her body trembled when I pulled her close, like she been waitin' just as long as me. Wasn't just lust. It was years of silence breakin' open, years of want crushed into one night. And I wanted more. Not just her body. I wanted her trust, her weight, her truth. I wanted her to look at me and know she ain't gotta carry it all alone no more.

Blinds shifted with a summer breeze, dust twistin' in the slice of light. Looked like a line cut through the room, and I knew exactly what side I stood on. The before was done. What came next—we claimin' that together. She don't gotta fight the world by herself, not while I'm breathin'.

I scooped my keys off the chair, metal cool in my palm. Malik's place was a roof for the night, but it wasn't home. I needed more than borrowed walls. I'd find it—a spot built for more than me, with space for Jaylah at the center. Hell, I could see her mama settled out back, safe and close. But before any of that, I had to get to her. Had to tell her straight, no room for doubt: she ain't need to stream no more. Not with me here. Not with the life I built for both of us waitin'. Not when every dream she buried could finally rise again.

The hallway smelled faint of dust and fried food from a neighbor's kitchen. My steps was steady, each one sealing the promise I made in the dark of a cell. By the time I saw her, she was gonna know the truth. Jaylah wasn't alone no more. I was home. And this time, I wasn't lettin' go.

The sun was already burning off the night when I rolled down her block, heat sitting thick on the brick like it owned the place. Kids cut across the cracked sidewalk, bike wheels rattling, chalk dust smudged on their knees. Old heads posted on the stoop, trading jabs about the game like they didn't have anywhere else to be. A lady two doors down fanned herself while watering a line of drooping plants. Same hood noise, same rhythm. I slowed up, parked a couple of spots away from her door, and let the engine tick itself quiet.

On the seat beside me sat a paper sack bleeding grease, biscuits soft and heavy, honey butter sweating through the cup. Two coffees rode shotgun too, sweet the way she always asked for. I scooped it all up, locked the car with my elbow, and climbed the steps with nothing but keys and intent.

Her door hadn't changed. Same soft gray, same little dent near the bottom from when she used to kick it open, juggling groceries. I tapped out a text.

I'm outside.

Didn't even get time to breathe before the lock clicked. She cracked the door and leaned in the frame, hair piled up messy, skin bare and shining, drowning in an old shirt with my number faded across the back. For a second, she just stared, then her eyes shifted like she was trying to believe I was really standing there. Not a phone call. Not a promise. Me.

"Roh." Her voice carried more weight than the sun.

"Morning." I held the tray up. "Got breakfast."

She didn't argue, just stepped back enough for me to move past. I slid inside like I never left, cool air brushing over my arms, the place smelling like vanilla and paper and her. She shut the door with her heel, arms folding tight across her chest like she had to remind herself to keep distance.

"You said you'd give me time," she said.

I set the food down and looked over my shoulder at her. "And you believed me?"

Her mouth tilted, almost a smile, almost a dare. "You don't mean half the shit you say."

I leaned against the counter, unwrapping a biscuit. "I mean every word. I just don't wait around on clocks that don't matter."

She tilted her chin, eyes glinting. "So you just decided to pop up."

"Decided you weren't gonna eat if I didn't put food in your hands." I slid the biscuit toward her. "Tell me I'm wrong."

She took it, lips twitching when the honey hit her tongue. "Cocky as hell."

"Confident," I shot back, grin tugging at the corner of my mouth. "You always liked that in me."

She rolled her eyes, but her laugh slipped through. "You're ridiculous."

I pushed off the counter, closing the space between us just enough to make her shift. "Nah. I'm necessary."

She bit her lip like she didn't want me to see her smile. "That's your line now?"

"You got a better one? Didn't see you telling me to get lost."

"Maybe I'm just being nice."

I let my gaze drop slowly to her mouth, then back up. "Nice, don't make you stare like that."

Her cheeks flushed, and she licked honey from her finger just to play with me. "You always had an answer for everything."

"Only when it's you." I let the words hang low between us. "Always been that way."

She shook her head, but the fight in her wasn't real. "You're trouble."

"Good thing trouble's exactly what you've been waiting on."

Her laugh cracked sharply, real, and her shoulders eased like she forgot she was supposed to guard herself. The tension thickened, humming between us. I reached out, caught her chin, lifted her face to mine.

"You gonna keep pretending you need time?" My thumb brushed her jaw. "Or you gonna admit you wanted me on this side of the door?"

Her pulse kicked under my hand. She didn't back away. "Maybe both."

"Then both belong to me," I murmured. "Your maybe and your yes. All of it."

Her lips parted, eyes locked to mine. "You don't fight fair."

I leaned in, voice rough in her ear. "Fair never won me a damn thing. But you? You're already mine."

When her mouth found mine, fast and hot, it felt less like a kiss and more like the truth snapping into place.

Her kiss hit me like a fuse, hot and reckless, her tongue pushing past my teeth while I caged her against the counter. My beard scraped her lips, and she gasped like she'd been starving for the taste of me. My hands locked on her hips, dragging her tight until there wasn't space for air between us. Six years with nothing but thoughts, and now I had her—I wasn't letting up.

She moaned into my mouth, nails clawing down my back. That sound—fuck, I'd chase it forever. I yanked her shirt up and off, eyes locking on the metal glint catching the light. Her nipples, pierced, perfect, tight peaks begging for my mouth. My grin cut sharply as I rolled one between my fingers, tugging until she gasped.

"Anybody play with these?" I rasped against her throat, teeth grazing her skin. "Or just you?"

Her breath shivered out. "Only me."

I sucked one into my mouth, tongue circling slowly before biting down hard enough to make her cry out. "Not anymore," I growled. "I'm gonna make you cum just from these."

Her back arched, her moan hitting the ceiling. I switched sides, sucking, pulling, biting until her thighs shook where they wrapped around me. My hand slid lower, under her shorts, fingers brushing the barbell at her clit, the metal cool against my touch. My chuckle vibrated against her skin. "And this? You hid this from me, too?"

She gasped, hips bucking into my hand. "Didn't think you'd like it."

"Baby," I said, thumb pressing hard over the piercing, rubbing tight circles while her legs trembled, "I fuckin' love it. You're gonna drip all over me while I play with this pretty pussy."

She whimpered, nails digging deeper into my shoulders. "Roh, please."

I dropped to my knees, shoving her shorts down and spreading her wide. I licked up her pussy slowly, teasing, before sucking her clit hard, letting the metal click against my tongue. Her scream shot through me, raw and sweet, and I pinned her thighs when she tried to squirm. "Don't run from me. You taste too good. I could stay between your thighs all night."

Her hands tangled in my beard, pulling me closer, grinding against my mouth. I slid a finger inside her pussy, then another, pumping deep, curling until her whole body bowed off the counter. She broke with a cry, pussy gripping my fingers while my tongue worked her clit until she couldn't breathe.

I pulled back, mouth slick, voice rough. "Turn around. Bend over."

Her legs shook as she obeyed, bracing herself on the counter. I spread her ass, leaned in, and licked her tight hole slowly, teasing. Her moan cracked open, shaky and high. "Roh—fuck—"

I tongued her deeper, spit dripping down, before sliding two fingers into her pussy again, working her open while my mouth ate her ass. She was crying now, begging, voice ragged. "Please, I need you, please."

I stood, freed my dick, and stroked hard against her soaked pussy. My hand tangled in her hair, yanking her head back. "You ready for me, Jay? 'Cause I'm not stoppin' till you can't stand up straight tomorrow."

"Yes," she breathed, wrecked and wild. "I want it."

That was all I needed. I shoved into her in one brutal thrust, balls slapping her clit piercing, and her scream ripped through the kitchen. I spanked her ass hard, the sound cracking, her pussy clenching tighter around me. "That's it, baby. Don't you dare hold back. I want every moan, every scream, every damn thing you feel."

She clawed at the counter, body bouncing under me, her voice breaking. "So deep—oh my God—"

"Good girl, taking me all the way," I growled, pounding

harder, teeth sinking into her shoulder until she shook. I slid a hand lower, circling her clit with my thumb, grinding the piercing into her nerve until she sobbed with pleasure.

Her body shattered around me, pussy clenching so hard it dragged my orgasm out of me. I pumped deep, groaning against her ear, spilling inside her while she trembled. I bit her throat, growling low, possessive. "You're mine everywhere—pussy, ass, all of you. Nobody else will ever touch you like this."

She sagged against the counter, sweaty and shaking, lips swollen and eyes glassy. I kissed her shoulder, chest still heaving. "That's mine, baby. Every bit of you."

five

TIDES TURNING

THE SPRAY HIT FIRST, BLISTERIN' hot the way I liked it, steam already foggin' the mirror outside the shower stall. It poured down my shoulders and chest in burnin' sheets, the kind of heat that always felt like it could strip the past off me. He was behind me, his big frame crowdin' the small space, one hand braced on the tile as he tested the water with a grunt.

"Still tryin' to melt yourself alive?" His voice was rough, tinged with amusement, but there was a thread underneath it, heavier than the laugh he tried to cover it with.

I smirked without openin' my eyes. "Some of us know what clean feels like, Roh. You wouldn't understand."

He pressed closer, chest to my back, his chuckle rumblin' low. The heat had to be stingin' him, but he stayed. "Clean? Baby, this ain't water. This fire."

I turned just enough to catch his face, the crooked smirk that used to be nothin' but a tease. Only now, with last night still echoing in my body, it was different. The kiss, the way he touched me like he'd been waitin' a lifetime, the way I let him take me without a single doubt. It wasn't just sex. It was somethin' that shifted everything I thought I knew.

I wanted to toss a joke back, keep it light. But the words stuck in my throat. 'Cause the truth was, in twenty-four hours, my world tilted. Yesterday mornin', I was alone, heavy with bills, streamin' for faceless men who only wanted parts of me I never wanted to give. Then he came back, flesh and bone, lookin' at me like I was worth more than every lie I'd sold to keep the lights on.

"You never liked the heat," I finally said, softer.

"Not this kinda heat." His gaze pinned me, steady, unshakin'. "But if it mean standin' here wit' you? I'ma take it."

My chest pulled tight, and I pressed a wet palm flat to the tile. He had a way of droppin' words that sounded casual but weren't. Not with him. Not after everything.

His hand settled at my hip, thumb strokin' lazy circles, not demandin', not pushin', just there. Groundin' me.

"Jay." The teasin' edge was gone from his voice now. "Talk to me."

I bit the inside of my cheek, steam chokin' the silence. "You scare me."

His grip firmed slightly. "Why?"

"Because you went away for me. Six years gone 'cause of one night, one fight that should've been mine to carry. And now you look at me like..." My throat caught. "Like I'm the best thing that ever happened to you, when all I've ever felt is guilt."

He turned me, slow but unyieldin', 'til I faced him fully. Water slid down his face, darkenin' his beard, runnin' over shoulders cut from years of survivin'. His jaw flexed, eyes burnin' hotter than the spray.

"Don't." His voice was steel. "Don't you carry that. I made my choice."

"But it was for me."

"It was for us." His hand came up, cuppin' my chin, makin' me hold his stare. "Don't twist it. I'd do it again, Jay. Every damn time."

The words tore me open. Tears blurred the steam, but I couldn't stop 'em. He brushed one away before it fell, his thumb firm against my cheek.

"You carried me in there," he said, voice breakin' low. "Your letters, the money, the way I could hear your voice in my head when the nights got too long. Don't you dare tell yourself you left me alone. You kept me alive."

My lips trembled. "I wanted to tell you everything. The bills, the rent, the streamin'. I wanted to—but every time I thought about you sittin' in that cell, I couldn't. You was already payin' for me, Roh. How could I give you more to carry?"

His palm slid to the back of my neck, anchorin' me in place. "Stop. Don't use that word again. You think it was punishment? Nah, baby, it was a purpose. You was purpose."

I shook my head, the water spillin' from my hair. "All I ever felt was guilt."

"Then feel this instead." He pressed his forehead to mine, steam curlin' between us. "I don't regret a single thing. What I regret is you thinkin' you had to hide from me."

The weight of his words pressed against every place I'd been cracked. For the first time in years, somethin' inside me loosened. I leaned into him, let it pour through me.

"I don't wanna hide no more," I whispered.

His lips brushed mine, tender, not claimin' but promisin'. "Good. 'Cause I ain't lettin' you."

We stood there, water scaldin', air thick, but it felt clean. Like maybe everything between us could burn down and still come out new. His hands slid over my arms, down to my waist, solid, remindin' me he was here. Not letters. Not calls. Him.

The water finally cooled, but neither of us moved 'til I reached past him and shut it off. The silence left was only broken by our breathin'.

He smirked then, the boy I remembered flashin' for a second. "So lava showers every mornin', huh?"

I laughed, raw but real, pushin' lightly at his chest. "Better get used to it."

He caught my hand, pressed it to his mouth. "After this mornin', baby? I'ma get used to anything."

And just like that, I saw him in a new light. Not just the boy from my past. Not just the man who went away for me. But the one standin' in front of me now, fierce and unshaken, ready to carry the weight with me instead of for me. For the first time, I believed it—we could be more than what broke us. We already were.

We left my apartment with the weight of morning still clinging to us, the air outside bright and restless. Roh's hand slid down my back as we walked to the car, his touch lingering like he couldn't stand even an inch of distance. He didn't say where we were headed right away, only, "Come ride wit' me," his tone low, carrying more certainty than question.

I arched a brow but moved with him easily. "Where to?"

"You gon' see," he said, opening my door and steadying me as I slid inside. The Charger was already hot from the sun, but his hand stayed warm and steady on my thigh after he climbed in. I didn't push him for more, not yet. His silence wasn't the kind that built walls—it was the kind that pulled me closer, made me want to wait and see what came next.

When he finally turned down a quiet side street, I realized what he was doing. Bookstores lined the block, some still alive, others sagging with For Lease signs in their windows. My chest tightened, both from the sight and from how easily he'd known where to take me.

He glanced at me, one corner of his mouth tugging upward. "Figured we could look 'round. See what feel right."

I tried not to let the sudden rush of excitement show, but it spilled anyway. Words started tumbling out before I could stop them—how I wanted the shelves wide enough for children to reach, how I imagined a section just for local authors, how the name Rooted Words made me feel grounded every time I said it. I talked about light, about chairs that invited you to stay, about tea jars and small press zines that deserved as much attention as the bestsellers.

I caught myself mid-sentence and shook my head, pressing my lips tight. "Sorry. I've said all this before. You don't need to hear me ramble again."

His hand tightened gently on my thigh, grounding me. "That's where you wrong," he said, eyes forward but voice sharp with truth. "I could hear you talk 'bout it a hundred times. Every detail. Every dream. Don't matter if you think you repeatin'—it always hit different to me."

I swallowed, nerves fluttering. "You really mean that?"

Finally, he turned to look at me, his gaze steady, burning. "Jay, your voice carried me through the worst parts'a prison. Not 'cause you asked for it. Not 'cause you even knew. But when I was ready to fold, I thought 'bout you. The way you argue, the way you laugh, the way you tell a story like the world gotta keep up wit' you. That's what kept me straight. You don't know how much it mean to hear you now. So don't stop. Not for me."

The air in the car felt thick, and I could barely keep my breath even. He didn't say it like a confession meant to weigh me down, but like a fact he wanted me to carry with pride instead of guilt. My chest ached from the force of it.

We parked in front of one of the quieter shops, the kind with old brick and tall windows clouded by age. Inside, the bell chimed faintly when we stepped through the door. The place wasn't busy, just a single clerk behind the counter scrolling through her phone, the smell of paper and dust rising all around. It felt private, like a world waiting for us to speak into it.

I drifted toward the shelves without thinking, fingertips grazing the spines of books I'd already read, already loved. Roh stayed close, always close, his presence a steady hum at my back. When I reached for a title to show him, he brushed up against me, his chest to my shoulder, his breath low in my ear.

"Keep talkin'," he murmured, lips grazing the shell of my ear. "Tell me everything. I wanna hear what this store s'posed to feel like when it's yours."

Heat flooded me, both from the words and the weight of him pressing against me. I tried to focus on describing it —the kids' corner with a rug shaped like clouds, the coffee bar in the back, the way I wanted every wall painted with color instead of left bare. But his hand slid to my hip, then lower, and my voice faltered.

I turned my head to give him a look, but he only

smirked, that rough edge to his smile. "Don't stop now. I told you, your voice do somethin' to me."

I laughed, soft and shaky. "You're impossible."

He leaned in until his lips brushed my hair. "You ain't got no idea how much I missed this. Hearin' you like this. Feelin' you like this." His dick pressed against my ass, the solid line of him unmistakable through our clothes. He rubbed slow, deliberate, like he wanted me to feel every inch of him.

My breath hitched, but I forced myself to keep speaking, if only because I knew that's what he wanted. "I want shelves that don't just hold books but invite people to stay. I want a table in the back where kids can draw or write. I want people to feel like they belong the second they walk in."

His grip on my waist tightened, and he kissed the side of my neck, beard scraping lightly. "That's it. Keep tellin' me. Let me hear how you see it."

I shivered, but I didn't stop. My words tumbled faster, spilling every piece of Rooted Words that lived in me. And every time I faltered, his voice was there, rough and certain, tellin' me to keep goin', that he could listen for hours.

When I finally fell quiet, catching my breath, he rested his forehead against my shoulder, his tone softer. "Whatever you want, Jay, I'm in it wit' you. However far you wanna take this—store, life, even the shit we do when we alone—I'm there. But only if you want it."

That last part made my pulse jump. I turned in his hold, searching his face. "You mean—kinks? Boundaries?"

He nodded once. "All that. I need to know how far you wanna go, what's off-limits, what's not. 'Cause I'ma give you every part'a me, but I ain't pushin' you nowhere you don't wanna be."

The honesty in his eyes left me raw. I swallowed hard. "I want it all, Roh. I want to know what we like together. I don't want to hold back."

His smirk curved slow, dangerous, but the heat in his gaze softened at the edges. "Good. 'Cause I plan on takin' you there. Every place we both wanna go."

We stood between the shelves, the hum of silence around us, our words heavier than any book in the room. For the first time, it felt like the future wasn't just an idea— it was already in motion.

six

THE OFFER

THE CITY SOUNDS different when you're free. Sirens fade quicker. Laughter hangs longer in the air. Even bass bumpin' from somebody trunk feel more like a heartbeat than noise. Sittin' across from Jaylah now, in the same booth I used to hold down with my elbows and a stack of napkins, all that sound felt like proof I made it back whole.

Leon's still the same. Same hand-painted sign above the door. Same cracked red vinyl that stick to your legs in the summer. Same chalkboard menu, prices rubbed out and written over so many times you could still see the old ones ghostin' underneath. Smell of hot oil and pepper hangin' in the air, catfish poppin' in grease, sweet tea sweatin' in mason jars. Leon got his old Falcons cap on, tilted like it was stitched to his head, and Miss Dee movin' through with a smile strong enough to make you forget the world outside still rough.

She saw Jaylah first, lit up. Then she clocked me and froze, hand pressed to her chest like she seen a ghost. "Boy," she said, voice droppin' low. "Look at God."

I stood up, hugged her tight. She squeezed harder than

bone should allow, then smacked my shoulder and told me don't make her cry at her job. When she walked away, she looked back twice, makin' sure I was real.

Our booth sat under the same crooked photo collage. Graduations. Little league squads. Leon and Miss Dee in sharp black and whites. At the end, a worn picture of two teens passed out shoulder to shoulder after a Saturday rush, fries between 'em, homework open. Me with a fade, no beard. Her with skinny brows and that smile she always tried to hide. Us.

Jaylah traced her finger down the condensation on her glass, smilin' without lookin' up. "You see us up there."

"I do."

"We were babies," she said.

I shook my head. "You been grown. I was just dumb."

She snorted, sipped, cinnamon still hangin' on her breath from earlier coffee. No matter what we ordered at Leon's, we always split lemon-pepper wings. Miss Dee brought 'em with extra napkins and a look like, behave. Wings came out steaming, lemon and pepper cuttin' the air. Jaylah reached first, like always, and I watched the shine hit her mouth.

"This place feel small now," she said after a beat. "Like the ceiling dropped while you were gone."

"It is small," I said, spreadin' my hands, "but it's ours. That's the difference."

She leaned back, eyes sweepin' the room, the families, old heads at the counter arguin' about a game long over. "We used to sit here after school, talk about everything like it was all comin' tomorrow."

"It still is," I told her.

Her eyes cut to mine. Something heavy moved between us.

Miss Dee slid back with catfish for me, shrimp and grits

for her, greens on the side, cornbread basket that could end arguments. She topped off our teas, gave me a look packed with six years' worth of mercy and joy, then left us.

I let the first forkful sit, eyes closed a sec. Seasonin', smoke, lemon heat. Prison turn food into fuel. This here tasted like life.

"You starin'," she said, pickin' at her food but not meetin' my eyes.

I smirked. "I was starving. Just catchin' up."

She let the quiet ride until I broke it. "Ain't think I'd make it back like this. Whole. Sittin' across from you."

Her gaze snapped up. "You was always gon' make it back."

I shook my head, thumb slidin' on the table till it brushed hers. "Nah, Jay. You don't know what it's like in there. Concrete get in you. Eats walls, food, air. Some men don't last. They get swallowed. But you—" my voice dropped, steady but rough—"you was my reason. Letters smelled like you. Notes 'bout books, seasons I couldn't touch. You thought you was just fillin' space. You gave me something solid. That's what carried me."

Her fork stilled. I kept on.

"You learn routine or it kill you. Wake to count, choke down meals you can't name, work your body so you don't break, keep your head low when fights pop. That rhythm get in your bones. But every night, I closed my eyes and heard you. Laughin'. Arguin' over some author. Dreamin' on that store. That sound kept me from losin' mine."

Her hand found mine, small but strong. "You make it sound like I saved you."

"You did. Not with no big moves. With steady truth. When the world shrank to a cell, you gave me a window. Don't mean it wasn't hell—I saw men lose years off their souls in there. But I held on 'cause I knew I'd walk out one day and find you. That thought turned ritual. Stronger than concrete."

Her eyes shined, but she gripped my hand harder. "I feel guilty. Like I should've done more. You're the only man who's ever looked at me like I'm more than the fantasy."

"Don't," I said, slidin' my hand full over hers. "You gave what I needed. Anything else would've been weight you ain't supposed to carry. Prison was mine to hold. The dream was yours to keep alive. Now we both here, standin' in the middle of it."

Her laugh came shaky, edged with tears she held back. "You always knew how to shut me up."

The laugh faded to quiet. She picked at her food again. I leaned back, elbows braced.

"Jay," I said, tone shifted. "I need you to hear me out."

Her eyes lifted slow, guarded. "That sound like trouble."

"Not trouble. Truth." I leaned in, voice low. "I ain't just survive inside. I built while I was gone. Invested. Stocks. Real estate. Had my brother runnin' it for me on the outside. Ain't flashy, but it stacked."

Her fork froze midair. "What are you saying?"

"I'm sayin' I'm good. Better than good." I sipped tea, calm, then dropped it plain. "I can fund Rooted Words. All of it. Storefront, stock, staff. No more piecin' scraps, no more stayin' up wonderin' which bill can wait."

Her fork hit the plate, eyes narrowin' like she tryna see through me. "You're serious."

"As a morning count," I said. "I ain't offerin' scraps. I'm talkin' makin' sure your dream breathe without it breakin' you down."

Her hand tightened round her glass. "And in exchange?"

"Nothing," I told her, truth sittin' clean. "This ain't control. It's payback. You kept me alive when I had nothin' but four walls and a voice on the phone. You don't know the weight of that. But I do. This me balancin' the scale."

Her shoulders went stiff. She shook her head slow. "I don't wanna be nobody's obligation. Or charity. That's not me."

I reached across, covered her hand, thumb slid on her knuckles. "And you not. This ain't charity. It's faith. You bet on me when nobody else would. Now I'm bettin' everything on you. That's partnership, not pity."

Her eyes flickered, wet but hard. She looked away, like Leon's walls closed in, ceiling droppin' low. "I just… I don't wanna lose myself in you."

"You won't." My grip tightened just enough. "This ain't me ownin' Rooted Words. It's makin' sure the world see what you built, without you killin' yourself to prove you can do it alone."

Her lips parted, but no words came. She let me hold her hand across the table, her pulse beatin' strong against my palm.

Miss Dee drifted past and topped off our teas without asking, eyes cutting between us like she could feel the shift in the air. She set a warm slice of pecan pie on the edge of the table and tapped the plate with her nail. "On the house," she said. "For courage." Then she was gone again, hips swaying to the old jukebox song humming in the corner.

Jaylah stared at the pie like it held an answer. Her shoulders stayed tight. I kept my hand over hers and waited. Silence can be a bluff or a bridge. I needed this one to carry us somewhere real.

"Say I agree," she said finally, voice low. "What does it look like tomorrow. Not in theory. In real steps."

"Tomorrow," I said, "you pick a lawyer who answer only to you. You pick an accountant too. I don't sit in them rooms unless you say so. Malik gon' send proof of funds to whoever you choose. I wire money to escrow that your lawyer control. First piece cover inspection, architect, and a contractor walk-through on whatever spot you want me to chase. Second piece lock your first inventory. Third piece sit for payroll and three months of cushion so you ain't opening with a clock ticking in your ear."

Her fingers twitched under mine. "And the store itself. Lease or buy."

"Your call," I said. "If you wanna lease to start, we take it with a renewal option and a purchase clause baked in at a number you cool with. If you wanna buy, we buy in cash and the deed go in Rooted Words LLC. Your name first. If you want me on the paperwork, it's as a silent note you can retire later. If you don't want me on it at all, I'm still paying. That part don't change."

She blinked slow. "So I could put you off paper and you would still fund it."

"Yes."

Her mouth pressed flat like she was testing the words against old fear. "That feels dangerous."

"It's only dangerous if you think I'm here to collect later," I said. "I ain't. I did six years thinking about what it mean to owe and be owed. I don't want that between us. I want you free in your head while you build."

She pulled her hand back and folded both on the table. "Then be honest. What do you want back from me."

"Nothing you don't wanna give," I said. "I wanna walk past your window and see families inside. I wanna hear a kid laugh in the corner 'cause he found a comic that look like him. I wanna watch you lock up at night and not see worry on your face. I wanna know you slept 'cause the bills ain't keep you up. If you asking for something I can write into a contract, write this. You keep control. You set the rules. If I get in the way, you say the word and I step back."

She held my eyes for a long beat. The room swelled with other people's talk and clatter, but none of it touched our table. "And me," she said soft. "Not the business. Me."

"You," I said, steady. "I want you 'cause I want you. Not 'cause of a store. Not to erase what happened. Not to put a crown on my head and say look what I saved. I want mornings where you burn the coffee and call it a roast. I want your mouth on mine when you happy. I want your mouth on mine when you mad. I want all the parts nobody else get."

Her breath left like something untied inside her. Then the fear came back around the edges and I saw it. She picked up her fork, set it down, then pushed the pie toward me. "You thought about all of this while you were inside."

"Every night," I said. "We had a little library. Old Business Week issues that still smelled like dust. One radio show that played after lights. Carter taught me how to read balance sheets on a scrap of paper we passed in church. Malik handled the deals. He kept it clean. He sent follow-ups when I couldn't. Lotta people do they time and fade. I did my time and built a lane so I wouldn't fade. I built it for me. I built it for us."

She swallowed. "And you think you can just lift my life out of the hustle I been living and set it here on a clean table like this. No mess. No sting after."

"No," I said. "I ain't arrogant. I know there gon' be mess. I know the first month you gon' feel like you falling. I know your hands gon' look for the camera the way mine still count the corner of a bed every night. Habits don't vanish 'cause you say the words. But I also know a safety net when I see one. Let me be that while your feet learn the new floor."

Her laugh cracked. Not mean. A little wild. She wiped at her eye and shook her head. "You talk like you wrote a manual."

"Only for you," I said.

The jukebox clicked and rolled into a slower song. Miss Dee slid a check on the edge of the table like she was trying not to intrude on a prayer. I reached for it and Jaylah reached too. Her fingers touched mine. She pulled back first.

"I'm paying," I said.

"You can buy my wings," she said quiet. "You can't buy me."

"I wouldn't try," I said.

We let that sit. I signed the slip and left cash for the tip so Miss Dee didn't chase me down with her eyebrows. When I looked up, Jaylah had her notebook out. The small black one she used for orders, ideas, lists, everything. She opened to a page full of numbers and little stars.

"These the real costs," she said. "Not the wish list. The minimums. Rent for a space that ain't a shoebox. Insurance. Point of sale. Wholesale starting orders for the authors I wanna carry out the gate. A part-time hire so I ain't sleeping behind the counter. Tea bar equipment. A story hour budget for the kids. Not fancy. Just honest."

She turned the notebook so it faced me and slid it across. I ran my finger down the columns while she talked. She explained each line without apology. I listened without interrupting. When I had a question, I asked it like she was the expert and I was the student. 'Cause she was and I wasn't.

"You missed your salary," I said after a minute.

She looked away. "I can wait on that."

"No," I said. "You won't. Put it in."

Her voice thinned. "Roh."

"Put it in," I said again. "The store don't eat you to live. That's the rule."

Her pen hovered. Then she wrote a number like it felt illegal. Her cheeks warmed. She ain't look at me. I wanted to kiss her for that alone. I kept my hands flat on the table and let her finish.

"Now add a small fund for local events," I said. "Pay your readers. Don't ask them to show up for exposure. Add a cushion for slow weeks. Add a marketing line that ain't just social. Flyers cost. Posters cost. Good photos cost."

She wrote the lines in tight print and sat back. "You always come in like this and take over."

"I ain't taking over," I said. "I'm building a wall around your time."

She watched me, chin tipped, eyes softer than before. "It feels like both."

"Then tell me where to stop," I said. "I'll stop there."

A long quiet stretched and didn't break. Finally she slid her notebook back to her side and closed it with a small snap.

"I need to say it out loud," she said. "I'm scared. Not of the money. Of the part where I let you carry something I told myself I had to carry alone. I told myself that for so long I carved it into my bones."

"I know," I said. "So I'm asking for a small thing first. Not forever. A trial. Give me two weeks where you don't stream. Just two. We take those days and move on the legal parts and the scouting and the schedule for suppliers. If at the end of two weeks you feel worse, you tell me and I'll find a way that don't touch your pride."

"One week," she said, eyes sharp.

"Ten days," I said.

She breathed out hard through her nose and a smile tried to show. "You're annoying."

"Ten days," I said again, softer.

She looked at her glass, then at me. "Okay. Ten days."

The words landed like a key in a lock. Something inside me eased. Not victory. Relief.

"Since we making terms," she added, voice steadying, "I want a clean line between us and the business. If this go left between you and me, the store stays mine. It don't collapse 'cause we do. That gotta be in writing."

"It will be," I said. "Your lawyer gon' write it. I'll sign it."

"And you don't touch my phone," she said. "Not a password. Not a peek. Not ever."

"I don't want your phone," I said. "I want your eyes when I talk to you."

Her mouth curved. "That's the kind of line that gets a girl in trouble."

"Then let it," I said.

We split the pie even though neither of us really wanted it. It felt like part of the rhythm inside this place that raised us. I boxed up her leftovers. She boxed up mine. Outside, hot air pressed against the door when we pushed through it, heavy and bright. The street noise hit and folded around us. She stood on the sidewalk and looked up at the same hand-painted sign I had looked at a thousand times before my life got measured in counts and lights out.

"You still sure," she said, not looking at me. "About all of this."

"I was sure before I sat down," I said. "I'm more sure now."

She slid her hand into mine. Not hesitant. Not rushed. Sure. I closed my fingers around hers and felt her pulse settle into mine.

"Take me home," she said.

"Yeah," I answered. "Home."

We walked to the car without another word. No grand promises on the pavement. No big speeches for the block to hear. Just her notebook tucked under her arm and my plan running quiet in my head. Ten days to build a runway. Ten days to teach her muscles a new reflex. Ten days to prove I meant what I said inside that booth. I started the engine, checked the mirror, and pulled into the slow roll of traffic. Her thigh touched mine and stayed there. That was enough for now.

seven

FAULT LINES

THE TAPE SCREECHED across another box, the sound grating in the small apartment. I pressed the strip down with the flat of my palm, the cardboard resisting for a second before it gave. The package slid into the growing stack by the door, a miniature wall I'd built out of the books wrapped in brown paper and bubble mailers. I should've felt accomplished. Orders meant people were still buying, still waiting on the handpicked titles, still trusting me to send them something that might shift their day. But instead of pride, all I felt was the drag of exhaustion in my shoulders.

Two days had passed since Leon's, but the conversation lingered like perfume caught in fabric. Roh's voice in that booth, steady and certain, replayed in my head every time the room got quiet. *I can fund Rooted Words—all of it.*

He hadn't said it like a question. He'd said it like a promise already signed in ink.

I folded packing slips, slid them into envelopes, but my mind wasn't on the work. It was back there at the table—his hand covering mine, the way his eyes didn't waver when I tried to joke my way out of the heaviness. Roh wasn't bluffing. I knew that down to the marrow. He'd told me about the investments, the way he built in silence while prison walls tried to close him in. His brother moving pieces outside, his patience stretching over the years. He wasn't the type to talk about dreams just to hear himself sound good.

And that was the problem.

The issue wasn't him. It wasn't trust. It wasn't even fear that he'd hold this over me later. The issue was me.

For so long, I'd built my life on the idea that if I didn't carry it, it wouldn't get done. Rent, Mama's medicine, my own little dream in the shape of a bookstore—it all sat on my back. Piece by piece, I'd learned how to juggle, how to stretch, how to make do. Sometimes it broke me down, sure. But it was *mine*. The struggle was the proof.

And now Roh was sitting across from me, offering to lift it all. To take the weight I'd taught myself to live under, to strip away the grind and the late nights and the endless calculations. Not because he thought I was weak. Not because he doubted me. But because he loved me enough to want me free.

I pressed another label onto a box, fingers trembling more than they should. Freedom sounded beautiful when I whispered it in my head, but in practice, it felt like surrender. It meant letting go of the only thing that had defined me all these years—my ability to carry, no matter how heavy.

The apartment was quiet except for the buzz of the fridge and the slap of tape against cardboard. My mind filled the silence with his words. *You don't get how much it means to hear you now.* The memory of his hand brushing over my knuckles across the booth. The way his voice softened when he called this faith, not charity.

I wanted to believe that. A part of me already did. But another part—stubborn, sharp, old as every sacrifice I'd made—kept whispering: if you let go, what's left of you?

I sat back, rubbing at my temple, eyes burning from staring too long at shipping forms. The vision board hung crooked above my desk, a mess of clippings and sticky notes I hadn't touched in months. Rooted Words spelled out in block letters. Coffee mugs, cozy corners, kids crouched on bright rugs. All of it taped with the desperation of someone who didn't know if they'd ever get there.

Now, suddenly, it wasn't impossible. Roh had placed the keys to that future right in front of me. All I had to do was take them.

And that terrified me more than any rejection, any failure.

Because taking them meant admitting I couldn't do it all alone. It meant trusting not just his love, but myself—to still be me if I wasn't struggling.

I thought about Mama, about the lines etched deep in her face from years of carrying too much herself. She'd taught me strength without saying the word. Watching her stretch meals, watching her swallow her pain so I could have one more chance, one more step forward. Letting go had never been part of the lesson.

But hadn't I wanted something different? Hadn't I sworn Rooted Words would be more than survival? A place to rest, a place to build, a place where the grind wasn't written into the walls? And wasn't that exactly what Roh was offering me?

The tape gun slipped from my hand, clattering against the table. I covered my face with both palms, dragging them down slowly, forcing air back into my lungs.

I wasn't scared of him. I was scared of how much lighter life could feel if I said yes.

Two days, and still my chest tightened every time I thought about it.

The kettle's whistle had just started to climb when the knock came. Three quick raps, a pause, then two more. Mama's rhythm, the same one she used when I was a kid and forgot my key. My chest loosened just hearing it.

I opened the door to find her standing there like she owned the hallway, tote bag hanging from one arm, lips pressed in a smile that said she already had a thought waiting.

"You gon' leave me out here like I'm a stranger?" she teased, brushing past me before I could answer.

I shook my head, smiling despite the tension riding me these last two days. "You know you don't need an invitation."

"Mm-hmm." She set the tote on the counter and started unloading like she lived here—collard greens, a bag of cornmeal, and that mason jar of bacon grease she kept like it was heirloom gold. "Lord, girl, this place looks like a post office. Boxes everywhere."

"Better than it looking empty," I said, sinking into a chair.

She gave me a pointed glance but didn't argue, just washed her hands and claimed the stove like it had been waiting on her. Soon, the kitchen filled with the crackle of bacon grease and the low hum of her humming. My throat itched with everything I wanted to say. About Leon's. About the way Kairoh leaned across the booth like no time had passed, how he'd put every excuse I had under a light and burned them down with a single truth: *I can fund Rooted Words.*

I wanted to tell her how the words had clung to me for two nights straight, circling, tugging, pulling me closer even while I tried to push back. Not because I didn't trust him. Not because I didn't want·him. But because I was scared of loosening my grip. Of not being the one carrying it all.

But Mama spoke first.

"That boy stopped by here the other day."

The spoon slipped from my fingers, clattering against the table. "What boy?"

She shot me a look sharp enough to cut. "Don't play with me. You know which boy. Well, not a boy anymore. A man. Walked in here like he never left. Bought me groceries, fixed that hinge on the back screen. Didn't even wait for me to ask."

Heat flushed my neck. "You didn't tell me."

"You didn't tell me he was home," she said, matter-of-fact, as she stirred the greens. "Imagine my surprise when my son-in-love shows up before my own daughter thinks to mention it."

My laugh came out shaky. "Son-in-love?"

"That's what he's been since you were teenagers. Don't act like I didn't see the way he used to look at you." She set the spoon down, leaned on the counter. "And don't act like you weren't looking back."

I tried to focus on the steam rising from the pot, but my heart was already racing. "It's not that simple, Mama."

"Baby, sometimes it is." She crossed the room and slid into the chair across from me, her eyes steady on mine. "That man walked out of prison, and the first place he came was to you. To check on me, to check on you. You think that's an accident?"

I pressed my lips together. The truth wanted to pour

out—about the dinner, the offer, the way he touched my hand across the table like he was staking a claim without ever raising his voice. About how I wanted to say yes, wanted to sink into the safety he offered, but was terrified of what it meant. If I let him carry this with me, was I still myself? Or just someone folded into him?

Mama's hand covered mine before I could sink too deep. "You're dying to talk about him. I see it in your eyes. So why you holding your tongue?"

My throat tightened. "Because if I start, I don't know if I'll be able to stop."

Her lips curved, soft and knowing. "Then maybe it's time you don't."

I stared at her, startled by the ease of it. She'd never pushed before, never said much beyond a raised eyebrow when his name came up. She let me live my choices, even when they tore me apart.

"I always wanted y'all together," she admitted, voice low but steady. "Always. I just never said it out loud 'cause love don't need a push. It needs space. But let me tell you plain: I prayed for him while he was gone. Prayed for you, too. And when I opened that door the other day and saw him standing there, looking like six years hadn't broken him, I knew my prayers had been heard."

Her words landed heavily. I thought of the way he looked at me in Leon's, steady, unwavering, as if he'd already decided where I fit in his life. And I thought of how my chest had swelled at the idea of Rooted Words being more than a dream I patched together paycheck by paycheck.

Mama squeezed my hand tighter. "Strength don't always mean carrying it all by yourself. Sometimes it means letting somebody else carry some of it with you."

I blinked fast, tears pressing at the corners of my eyes.

"But if I let him—" My voice cracked. "If I let him, doesn't that mean I couldn't do it on my own?"

She shook her head slowly, firmly. "Baby, you already proved you can do it on your own. You kept this family standing. You paid bills, kept lights on, took care of me when it should've been the other way around. You done carried enough weight to break anybody else. You don't have to keep proving the same thing forever."

The kettle screeched, but I barely heard it. My chest felt split open, all the words I'd buried spilling loose inside me. I thought about nights when I'd prayed too, asking for a break, a breath, a way forward. Maybe Kairoh was that answer. Maybe he always had been.

Mama stood, poured the hot water into a mug, and slid it in front of me. Her smile was gentle now, almost teasing. "Besides, you think I'm blind? I saw the way you floated in here after that dinner. Don't tell me it was just shrimp and grits making you smile like that."

I laughed wetly, shaking my head. "You're impossible."

"And you're in love." She said it plain, without hesitation. "Ain't no shame in that, Jay. Just means you finally letting yourself breathe."

The apartment felt cavernous once the door clicked shut behind Mama. For all her teasing and warmth, she always managed to leave a silence in her wake, one that made me face what I had been dodging. The kitchen still smelled like bacon grease and collards, the steam from the pot curling along the ceiling. I stood there a long time staring at the counter, my hands braced against it like it was the only thing holding me steady.

Her words kept replaying, looping with no exit ramp. *Strength don't always mean carrying it all yourself.* Easy to say when you had someone to lean on. Harder when you'd built your whole identity around proving you didn't need to.

But the truth was right there, heavy in my chest. I wanted him. Not just for the way he offered to fund Rooted Words, not for the practical safety net of his money or muscle. I wanted him because every time I thought of his voice, his eyes across the booth at Leon's, the way he reached across the table and held my hand like no time had passed, my body lit up. I wanted to give him something in return, to show him I saw what he had done, what he was still offering without asking for anything but me.

My phone sat on the counter, black screen reflecting my frown until I finally grabbed it. My thumb hovered longer than I wanted to admit before I hit his name.

"Jay?" His voice poured through the speaker, deep, steady, tinged with surprise.

I cleared my throat. "You busy?"

"Nah, mama. Just sittin' here, thinkin' 'bout you." The grin was audible.

Heat slid up my neck. "Can you come over?"

The pause was brief but thick, like he was reining himself in. "Say less. I'll be there in ten."

I spent those ten minutes pacing the apartment, smoothing the throw on the couch, fluffing pillows, then tossing them back down because it felt ridiculous. My nerves had me buzzing like I'd just downed three espressos. By the time his knock came, my pulse was beating everywhere—neck, wrists, thighs.

He filled the doorway the second I opened it, broad

shoulders blocking out the hall. His gaze swept over me, slow and hungry. "You lookin' at me like you don't know if you wanna kiss me or run."

"Maybe both," I whispered.

"Good," he said, stepping in close, his scent—clean soap, smoke, something darker—crowding my lungs. "Keeps it interestin'."

I didn't wait for him to close the door. I kissed him first, hard, desperate, teeth clicking against his before he angled his mouth to claim me back. His hands slid down my waist, gripping my hips tight enough to make me gasp. He pulled back just enough to murmur against my lips, "I knew it. You been missin' me just as bad."

The admission tumbled out before I could catch it. "Worse."

His chuckle was low, rough. "Then let me fix that."

We stumbled toward the bedroom, his hands everywhere, stripping away hesitation with every touch. When I pushed him back on the edge of the bed, he let me, a flicker of surprise flashing in his eyes before he grinned wide, teeth sharp in the low light.

"You tryna take charge tonight?"

"Just for a minute," I said, sinking to my knees between his legs.

His breath hissed when I took him in my mouth, slow at first, savoring the weight and heat of him. My tongue curled around him, spit slipping down my chin. His hand tangled in my curls, guiding my rhythm as his voice dropped to that dangerous growl that made me wetter.

"Look at you," he muttered, thumb brushing my cheek as he pushed deeper. "Messy for me… I love seein' you like this. Mouth full of me, eyes waterin'—that's my filthy girl."

I moaned around him, the vibration making him buck harder. I spat on him, stroked, then swallowed him again, throat working until he pulled me back suddenly, breath ragged.

"Hold up. If you keep doin' that, I'mma nut right here. And I need to be inside you when I do."

The words hit me like fire. He yanked me up and kissed me, wet and sloppy, before flipping me onto the bed. His mouth trailed down my neck, sucking at the spot that made me arch, before spreading my thighs wide. The first stroke of his tongue made my back bow clean off the mattress. A moan slipped from my mouth.

"That's right, Jay Baby. Keep making those sexy little noises. I wanna the whole block to know I'm makin' you mine."

I couldn't have stayed quiet if I tried. He devoured me, tongue and lips relentless until I was clawing at the sheets, begging for more.

With a low growl, he pushed up over me, the head of his dick sliding against my soaked folds before he sank inside, deep into my ass.

Relax, baby," he murmured, his breath hot against me. "I'mma make you take it all."

My cry tore loose as he filled me, every inch stretching me wider, until my nails dug crescents into his shoulders. He reached for the rabbit vibrator on the nightstand and pressed it into my hand.

"Hold that toy in while I fuck you deeper," he commanded, thrusting, punctuating every word. "Don't drop it, mama, or I'll start over."

The sensations tore me apart—the toy buzzing, his dick filling my ass, every movement hitting nerve endings I didn't know could sing. My voice broke, his name spilling out like a prayer.

When I came, it was violent, my whole body convulsing, pussy clamping the toy while my ass gripped him.

He didn't stop, his hips moving in a relentless rhythm, drawing out my orgasm until I was begging for mercy.

"Roh, please... I can't take any more," I gasped, my body trembling.

He chuckled, a dark, dangerous sound. "You can and you will. I'm not done with you yet."

He flipped me onto my stomach, pulling my hips up until I was on my knees. He entered me from behind, his hands gripping my waist as he drove into me with deep, powerful strokes. The angle was perfect, hitting that spot inside me that made stars explode behind my eyes.

"Fuck, you feel so good," he groaned, his voice strained. "So tight, so wet. You're gonna make me cum so hard."

I pushed back against him, meeting his thrusts, my body coiled tight with anticipation. He reached around, his fingers finding my clit, rubbing in tight circles that had me seeing stars.

"Cum for me again, Jay Baby," he commanded, his voice a low growl. "Let me feel you cum all over my dick."

I obeyed, my body shattering into a million pieces, my pussy clenching around him as I came undone. He followed me over the edge, his hips stuttering as he filled me with his release, my name a low, guttural moan on his lips.

We collapsed onto the bed, our bodies slick with sweat, our breaths coming in ragged gasps. He pulled me close, his arms wrapping around me, holding me tight.

"Mine," he murmured, his voice a low rumble. "Always mine."

I smiled, snuggling closer, my body sated and my heart full. "Yours," I whispered back, drifting off to sleep in his arms.

eight

ROOTS AND BRICKS

THE MORNING SAT warm on the curtains when I woke up, soft light pulling the edges of the room into focus. Jaylah slept on her side, one hand curled under her cheek, hair fanned across my pillow like dark water. I watched her breathe for a moment and let it settle me. Last night had burned through every wall I had left. This, right here, was the cool that came after. Quiet. Certain. The kind of quiet that makes a man get up and go make things happen.

I slid from the bed without taking the covers with me and eased my feet to the floor. The boards gave a small complaint under my weight. She stirred, lashes fluttering, then sank again. I bent and pressed my mouth to her shoulder, tasting the faint salt of sleep and soap. "Rest, mamas," I whispered into her skin. "I got moves to make."

The words sat true in my chest. They weren't about running the streets, proving myself, or stacking paper just to see the numbers climb. This was different. Purposeful. She had shifted something in me, and now I needed to meet that shift head-on.

I showered quickly, the water snapping me awake as

my thoughts lined up like soldiers. Jaylah's laugh echoed in the back of my mind, the way she'd whispered my name when she broke apart under me. I carried that into the mirror, into the crisp shirt I pulled over my shoulders, into the shoes I laced with a tightness that matched the set of my jaw. By the time I grabbed my keys, the softness of the bed had faded, leaving me sharpened.

The hallway outside smelled faintly of old paint and somebody's breakfast frying. The city was already warming up, buses groaning down the block, kids calling out on their way to school. I walked through it with my chest lighter, like the rhythm of the world matched the beat inside me for the first time in years.

I hit the corner café and picked up two coffees, two egg-and-cheese croissants. One for me, one for Malik. My brother always said breakfast was a man's first investment in the day. I figured I'd cover the overhead.

The office was still the same cramped setup we'd been using for months, but stepping inside felt like entering a different arena altogether. Monitors glowed with tickers, charts, red and green flashes racing each other down the screen. Whiteboards leaned against walls, half-cleaned equations standing ghostlike behind new scribbles.

Malik sat in the middle of it all like a conductor, chair leaned back but eyes sharp, scanning three screens at once with his phone in his hand. He glanced up as soon as I walked in, lips curling in a smirk.

"You late."

I set the bag down between us, slid the cup toward him. "Not late. Strategic. Coffee-and-croissant strategy."

He chuckled, took the cup. "Mm. You only this generous when something's on your mind." His look lingered a second, a knowing glint in it. "Must be good, 'cause you walking in lighter than usual."

I powered up my station, screens brightening to the hum of early trades. "Maybe I am."

"Yeah," he said, sipping slowly. "Feels like you finally decided what lane you driving in. 'Bout time, little brother."

"What's new is I'm done halfway-livin'," I said, keying in quick on a shipping stock slipping off the bell. Hold, count, sell. Profit stacked neatly. Malik whistled low.

"Clean. Pops woulda have liked that." He took a bite, chewed, and pointed with the sandwich. "And he'd like seein' you steady about somethin'—or someone."

I let that ride without answering, but the silence said enough. Malik didn't press, just grinned like the scoreboard already proved him right.

"I'm buildin' behind it," I said finally.

"That's the line right there." He washed it down with coffee, eyes back on the tape. "So what you need from me today—besides keeping the books pretty?"

"Paperwork in motion for her store, proof of funds to her lawyer, soft list on three storefronts with good bones. And I'ma start lookin' at houses. Backyard, room for folks to land."

Malik's grin widened. "Now you talkin' roots. We'll line the money clean, same as always." He leaned back, eyes narrowing just a little. "And if she's the reason you waking up sharper, then good. That's the kinda reason worth putting bricks on top of."

We worked in rhythm for the next hour—numbers shifting, headlines updating, both of us moving like we'd rehearsed it for years. He flagged a freight note; I cut the position before the market caught wind. Another clean win.

"You listening sharper these days?" he said.

"I ain't got time not to."

He tapped the desk. "Good. 'Cause once you sign

those papers, there ain't no part-time builder. Close the store, then the house. Keep that woman smiling. That's your whole job description."

"Bet."

He clapped my shoulder, heavy and proud. "Glad you're finally acting like it."

By noon, our numbers gleamed. He crumpled the wrapper, tossed it. "Lunch?"

"Always."

We stepped into the sun, city noise rushing us like a tide. For once, I wasn't running to catch it. I was setting the pace—with my brother at my side and Jaylah at the center of where I was headed.

I left the office with numbers still humming in my head and Malik's last word sitting heavy in my chest. Build. Not talk. Build. Sun sat high but soft, the kind of light that makes everything look like a start instead of a mess. I pulled out my phone before I hit the corner.

"You awake, mamas?"

Her answer came quickly, voice warm like fresh sheets. "I am now."

"Good. You got an hour in you? Put somethin' pretty on. I wanna show you a couple of things."

She laughed, low and pleased. "You bossin' me around again."

"I'm invitin' you," I said. "Whole different thing."

"Fine," she said, and I could hear the smile. "I'll be ready."

"Text me your tea order," I added, already angling

toward the florist at the end of the block. "And don't argue."

"You already know it. And I don't argue," she said, lying and knowing I knew. Then softer, "Hurry up."

I pocketed the phone and pushed into the little shop that stayed cold even in July. The air smelled like green things and wet stems. I pointed at sunflowers big as plates, a handful of white ranunculus, a stem of eucalyptus for the clean bite. The lady wrapped them slowly while I watched the street. When she tied the ribbon, I dropped cash, nodded thanks, and cut back to the car.

Jaylah was on the steps when I pulled up, sunlight catching her ankles and the edge of her smile. Hair loose, a soft dress that moved when she did, lips glossed like she had plans for them. I took a breath I did not know I needed.

"These are for you," I said, holding out the bouquet. "Figured your spot could use some happiness in a jar."

She tucked her face into the petals, eyes closing for a second. "They're perfect."

"You look better," I said, because I do not do speeches when the truth is simple. "Come on."

She slid in, set the flowers gently on her lap.

"Where are we going?" she asked, buckling in.

"Stops," I said. "First one is tea, 'cause I know you'll turn to smoke without it. Second is houses. Third is a door you're gonna like."

Her brow wrinkled. "Houses."

"Yeah," I said, turning the corner. "I'm done with borrowed walls. Time to get somethin' with a backyard and a porch swing where you can talk mess about the neighbors."

She shook her head, smiling into her cup when I

handed her the tea at the drive-up. "You really move like that, huh?"

"I don't move," I said. "I choose."

The agent met us outside the first place, a neat little bungalow with fresh paint and a yard that tried hard. He stepped down from the porch, bright smile, folder in hand.

"Mr. Reeves, good to finally meet you."

"It's Kairoh," I said, grip firm so we set the tone right. "This is Jaylah."

"Of course," he said, recalibrating fast. "I've got three today that hit most of your notes. Light, storage, quiet block, not far from her mama's."

"Let's walk," I said.

Inside was pretty. New counters. Shiny floors. Windows that let the morning fall straight across the living room. Jay ran her hand along the trim like she wanted to learn its shape. I watched her more than I watched the house.

"I like the light," she said.

"Me too," I said, crouching to look at a vent, then at the baseboards where paint had dripped lazily. "But the bones ain't talkin' loud enough. Smell that?"

She sniffed, confused. "Paint."

"Paint coverin' something," I said. I tapped the wall near the back door with my knuckles. "This corner had water. I can hear it."

The agent started to protest, then stopped, following my line of sight to a hairline wave near the base. "We can get a report on that."

"Get it," I said. "But don't get attached."

Outside, a neighbor kid shot a hoop against a bent rim and nodded at us like we were already home. Jay smiled and waved back. I filed the look on her face away. Not this house. But that look was the target.

The second house sat two blocks over, brick with a

porch big enough to hold a summer. The screen door creaked just right. Inside, the air felt lived in even though it was empty. Old wood floors, steady under my feet. A kitchen that begged for late-night plates.

Jay stood in the middle of the room and turned slowly. "It feels like people laughed here."

"That's a good sign," I said. I opened cabinets. Looked under the sink. Checked the crawlspace hatch. No damp. No mold. A little dust, like the house had been waiting politely for somebody to claim it.

She walked to the back door and looked out at a yard with a crooked oak and a patch of dirt that could be a garden if somebody loved it. "I can see Mama on that porch," she said softly. "I can see kids at that tree."

"Good," I said. "Put this one in the keep pile."

We stood together in the doorway to the primary bedroom, light slanting across the floorboards. She leaned into my side without thinking, and I let my hand drop to her waist because there was no reason to pretend it did not belong there.

"Roh," she said, quiet enough that the agent could not catch it. "We can do this."

"We are already doing it," I said. "And while I'm sayin' what's true, I'm paying off your mama's house this month. I made a call. Ain't nobody calling her askin' for one more dime. She done carried enough."

She froze, eyes wide and wet around the edges. "You did what?"

I kept my voice even. "Handled it. You took care of mine when I ain't have a window. I take care of yours. Balance, mamas."

Her chin trembled. She fought it, then lost, a tear slipping hot and quick. I thumbed it away, no shame in it. The agent pretended to check his phone so we could have the moment.

"You keep making me believe this is easy," she whispered.

"It ain't," I said. "But it's simple."

We hit the third house because the agent insisted. New build. Tall ceilings. Cold as a hotel, even with the sun pouring in. Everything is white and hard. Jay lasted two rooms.

"This feels like a staged photo," she said, already backing up.

"Next," I told the agent, and we were gone.

She tucked the flowers deeper into the back seat so they would not cook in the heat. "You said there was a door I would like," she reminded me, eyes curious.

"Yeah," I said, turning past a block with a mural that looked like it had been painted on a dare. "You sent me that spot before. Said it had a vibe."

We rolled up a minute later. Old brick like a good book spine. Tall windows dressed in dust. Black iron handles on double doors that needed oil and respect. The sign space above the transom was blank. I saw her name there without even trying.

Jay went quiet as she took it in. Not a scared quiet. A reverent one. She stepped out before I cut the engine and stood on the sidewalk looking up, eyes bright, mouth parted like she had caught a miracle in the wild.

"This the one," I said, even though she had not said it yet.

"It could be," she answered, voice soft like she might spook it away if she got too loud. "Look at the front. Look at the bones. There is room for a kids' corner and a table for workshops, and a wall for local authors. The back could hold a tea bar. The light comes in right where I would put the new releases."

The agent jogged over with a key and a disclaimer about dust and original fixtures. I waved the words off and pushed the door open. Air moved, stale at first, then settling into something that smelled like old paper and chance. Not a bad smell. A promise smell.

We walked slowly. She trailed her fingers over a scarred counter like she was learning its language. I measured with my eyes, counted outlets, and checked the slope of the floor. There was a dip near the back that a good crew could handle in a day.

She stopped in the middle and turned to me, both palms flat on my chest. "Can we really do this?"

I set my hands over hers. "We already are. You say the word, I wire escrow. Your lawyer gets the docs. The architect walks it this week. I want you holdin' keys by the time school starts back."

The agent cleared his throat, eager. "There are two competing inquiries. If you want it, we need to move."

"We movin'," I said. "Price point, contingencies, inspection timeline. Send all of it to her counsel. And call me Kairoh."

"Got it," he said, scribbling. "Kairoh."

I looked back at Jay. "Walk me through it. Where you want the front table?"

She lit up in that way that makes my chest loosen. "Here," she said, dragging me three steps right. "New releases. A display that makes people stop and touch them. Kids corner there, under the window, so the sun hits the rug in the afternoon. Local authors along that wall. A little stage right here for readings. Then back there, tea, nothing too loud. Warm. Comfort. Belonging."

"Say less," I murmured, even as she kept talking. I

wanted to memorize the way her hands painted the air, the way her eyes cut to the door like she already saw the bell tied with ribbon, the way she stood in the middle of that empty room like a person who had finally been recognized by the dream she named.

When we stepped out, she leaned into me and looked up at the blank signboard above the doors. The street noise rolled around us like usual. For me, it went low. Focused.

"What do you see when you look up there?" I asked.

"My name," she said, not shy now. "Rooted Words."

"Good," I said. "I see it too."

We grabbed plates from a truck two blocks down. She ate standing up, napkin tucked against her wrist, eyes still on the building like she was afraid it might walk away if she blinked. I wiped a smear of sauce from her lip with my thumb, and she caught my hand and kissed the pad of it. Nothing loud. Everything final.

"I'm proud of you," she said.

"I'm proud of us," I answered. "And I ain't done."

I took her to her mama's after, because I like dropping blessings at the feet of the people who raised her. I walked them both through what was already in motion. Her mama tried to argue about the house note. I told her the same thing I told Jay. Balanced. Finished. Handled. She looked at me a long time, then pressed my face between her palms and told me God had a sense of humor.

On the way back, Jay slid her hand over the console and laced our fingers. City heat pressed against the glass. Her flowers rustled in the back seat every time we hit a light.

"You feel different," she said finally. "Not brand-new. Just settled."

"'Cause I am," I said. "I found what I was workin'

toward and gave it a name. You. Home. That store. And I don't plan on losin' any of it."

She turned her face and looked at me like she was measuring the weight of the truth. Then she nodded, small but sure. "Okay, Kairoh."

"Okay, mamas."

When I parked, I cut the engine and stepped out first, circling to her side. She looked at me, surprised, but smiled when I opened her door like it was the most natural thing. The bouquet shifted in her arms as she stood, bag slung over her shoulder, dress catching the evening breeze.

"Come on," I said, hand at the small of her back as I walked her up the steps. The building smelled faintly of rain on brick, the kind of scent that clings after the city cools.

At her door, she turned to me, flowers pressed tight to her chest, eyes soft in the low light. "You didn't have to walk me up."

"I wanted to," I said, leaning closer. "I need to know you made it inside before I roll."

Her lips curved. "You're impossible."

"And you love it."

She laughed, quiet but real, then tipped her chin up. I kissed her slowly, steadily, not rushed, sealing everything we'd just put in motion. When I pulled back, her eyes lingered on me like she wasn't ready to let go.

"Text me when you get home," she said.

"I will. And Jay?"

"Yeah?"

"You got me. Every way."

Her hand brushed mine before she turned the key. I waited until the door closed behind her before I walked back down the steps. The street noise picked up again, but it didn't touch me. Not tonight.

nine

CLEAN BREAKS

THE FLOWERS WERE STILL HOLDING their color. Sunflowers tilted toward the light on my windowsill, eucalyptus trailing long and steady over the lip of the vase. Every time I caught their scent, it carried me back to that afternoon with him—the way Kairoh pressed them into my hands like it was nothing, even though I knew better. He had a way of making gestures heavy and light at the same time, like the world could turn on a dime but only if you were brave enough to claim it.

It had been a few days, but the feeling lingered. Not that anxious rush that used to tie my stomach in knots when I let someone close. Not the voice in my head whispering about strings, traps, and debts I'd never shake free from. This was different. Steady. Solid. Like I'd been poured into instead of drained. Like the weight I carried didn't vanish, but shifted—shared.

The apartment looked different, too, though nothing had moved. Flowers on the sill. Papers spread across the table in neat stacks instead of frantic piles. My laptop is glowing, its screen covered in tabs: lease estimates, renovation costs, contractor contacts. Next to it sat the notebook where I'd been sketching layouts—shelves tall enough to hold everything from children's picture books to hardbacks, a corner rug for story hours, a chalkboard wall with "Rooted Words" painted bold across the top.

I traced one of my sketches with the edge of my nail, my chest lifting in something like pride. For once, I wasn't calculating which bill could wait, which corner I could cut. I wasn't surviving. I was planning. Building. Dreaming in blueprints instead of in scraps. That felt like a luxury I hadn't realized I'd been starving for.

The soft buzz on the edge of the table pulled me from my thoughts. I barely glanced at the phone, already expecting one of Kairoh's quick texts—on my way, you good?—but the name on the screen froze me.

Rodney.

The letters looked jagged now, like graffiti that should've been painted over long ago. My thumb hesitated, then curiosity got the better of me.

Funny how he took the fall for you. Bet he doesn't even know the whole story. You always was good at playing the victim.

The words hit sharp, aiming straight for the old wounds. For a second, muscle memory flared: chest tight, breath locked, that familiar panic that used to curl me small whenever his voice filled a room. Rodney knew how to twist guilt into chains. He'd done it for years.

But the feeling burned out almost as fast as it came.

I read it again, then leaned back in my chair. He really thought he still had a hold? That he could spit poison into my peace and make me stumble?

A laugh slipped out—dry, but real. He didn't scare me. He didn't shame me. He just annoyed me.

Rodney had once been the kind of man I mistook for steady. He called it holding me down, but really, he held me back. Every dream I spoke out loud, he cut down until it felt ridiculous. "Bookstore?" he'd laughed once, like I'd told him I wanted to buy the moon. "Girl, you barely keep your lights on." Back then, I believed him—believed that smallness was realism. Until his words pressed so deeply into my skin, I stopped speaking dreams out loud at all.

Now, with sketches spread across my table and sunlight spilling across plans that were becoming real, I knew better.

Rodney's next message lit the screen. *Bet you had him on the phone while I was at work. Bet you laughin' at me now.*

The same accusations. The same tactics. Only this time, I didn't scramble to defend myself. I didn't type back three paragraphs begging him to believe a truth he was never interested in. I just let my eyes skim over the words— then hit delete.

Gone.

Let him cling to his story if it made him feel bigger. Let him spit my name in circles that didn't touch me anymore. None of it reached me. Not now.

My hand tightened around my pen, and I bent back over my notebook. The scratch of ink against paper drowned out the last of his voice in my head. A shelf line stretched into a counter, into a corner rug, into a place where children would laugh and learn. That was real. That was mine.

Another buzz rattled the table. I didn't check it. Instead, I poured myself more tea, letting the steam curl against my face. The old me would've folded—would've picked up the phone, pleaded, tried to explain. But that girl was gone.

The woman sitting here now understood silence could be a weapon, too.

I looked up, the flowers catching my eye again. Still

bright. Still standing. Just like me. And I realized Rodney wasn't a threat. He was a reminder.

Proof of how far I'd come.

I turned back to my notes, fingers moving as quickly as I typed a list of contractors to call first thing tomorrow. My phone buzzed again. I didn't so much as glance at it.

Rodney could shout into the dark all he wanted. I was too busy building something that would outlast every bruise, every scar, every word he ever tried to pin on me.

By the time I closed my notebook, the table was cluttered with plans and sketches. And at the center of it all, the flowers.

Bright. Lasting. Mine.

I slid the last padded envelope into the blue box at the corner, pressing it down until it disappeared with the rest. My arms ached, but it was the good kind of ache—the kind that said work had been done, orders shipped, progress made. I pulled my bag higher on my shoulder, already thinking about the notes waiting on my desk, when the air around me shifted.

That's when I saw him.

Rodney.

Leaning against a dented gray sedan across the street, like the years hadn't touched him. Low hat, a glint of chain catching the sun, arms crossed over his chest as if he had all day to wait. The smirk on his face was the same one I remembered too well—mocking, sharp, a smirk that had once made me second-guess myself until I shrank.

For a half second, my chest pulled tight, the old reflex trying to rise: defend, explain, freeze. But it passed. Quick.

I didn't let him catch my stare for long. Didn't let him think I was standing still. My feet moved before my brain finished the thought, climbing the steps two at a time. The key was already in my palm by the time I reached my door, my breath fast but steady. Lock turned, bolt slid, door shut.

I leaned against it, spine pressed to the wood, one hand braced on the knob as if that alone could hold back the past. My phone burned in my pocket. I pulled it out and hit Kairoh's name without hesitation.

He answered on the first ring. "Jay? You good?" His voice was low, clipped—alert.

I swallowed hard, then made myself say it plain. "He's outside."

Silence on the line. Heavy. I could hear his breath shift, sharper. "Who?"

"Rodney," I whispered, the name tasting like rust. "He's leaning on a car across the street. I—I don't want you to come out swinging, Roh. I just needed you to know. I need you here, but I need you steady."

His inhale cracked loudly in my ear. Then he exhaled slowly, measured. "You did right tellin' me. I'm on my way."

"Kairoh—"

"I hear you," he cut in, voice rough but anchored. "I ain't gon' do nothin' stupid. But you lock that door, you hear me? Stay inside till I get there."

I nodded even though he couldn't see it. "Okay."

"Good. Fifteen minutes." His tone softened, the edge thinning just enough to reach me. "Ain't nobody touchin' you again, mama. Not now, not ever."

The call ended, but my pulse stayed high. I leaned against the counter, flowers still standing tall on the sill, and let the weight of it settle. I hadn't just told him Rodney was back. I'd handed him a piece of my past I swore I'd buried.

And for the first time, I believed it wouldn't break us.

I couldn't sit. Couldn't read. Couldn't force myself back to the sketches waiting on the table. The only thing I could do was pace from window to wall, then back again, every nerve stretched thin.

When the sound of an engine cut low on the block, I knew. My feet carried me fast to the window, fingers parting the curtain just enough to see.

Kairoh's car eased up to the curb, his frame unfolding from the driver's seat with that same weight I'd watched him carry since we were kids. He didn't rush. He didn't stalk. He just walked—steady, heavy, a presence you couldn't mistake even from across the street.

Rodney straightened off the sedan, arms dropping, smirk tilting wider like he thought this was his show. He said something I couldn't hear, but his shoulders moved with it—mocking, baiting.

Kairoh didn't bite. He stopped just short, close enough that his voice carried when he spoke, low but hard.

"Stay the hell away from her."

Even muffled through glass, his tone hit deep, dangerous in its calm. He stepped closer, chin lifted, every inch of him a warning.

"You hear me, Rod? Whatever you think you got left here, it's done. You don't call her, you don't text her, you don't show your face on this block again. 'Cause next time, I ain't talkin'."

Rodney barked out a laugh, loud and hollow. But even from here I saw it—the way his weight shifted back, the way his eyes flicked around like he was checking who was watching. His mouth kept moving, but the bite was gone.

Kairoh leaned in, close enough that only Rodney heard the next part. My stomach twisted, but Rodney's face told me enough: the grin slipped. He looked smaller. Shook his head like he wanted to argue, then thought better of it.

Kairoh didn't lay a hand on him. Didn't need to. He just stood there, steady as a wall, until Rodney cursed under his breath, yanked open his car door, and peeled off down the block.

I let the curtain fall, chest heaving. Relief rushed me so fast my knees wobbled.

A minute later, heavy steps sounded on the stairs. Then the knock—three beats, firm, familiar. My hands shook as I unlocked the door.

He filled the frame, jaw tight, eyes still burning from what he'd just walked through. But the moment his gaze landed on me, it softened.

"You good?" he asked, voice low.

I nodded, but the tears I hadn't meant to cry welled up anyway. He stepped inside, closing the door with one hand while the other reached for me. I folded into him, his chest solid under my cheek, his arms wrapping around me like a fortress.

"He gone," he murmured into my hair. "Ain't comin' back. Not while I'm here."

I clutched his shirt, let the weight of him anchor me. And for the first time in years, I believed it—believed I wasn't standing alone against the past anymore.

We lingered at the table longer than the food required, forks idle, conversation stretching easily between us. When the plates were empty, Kairoh stacked them and carried them to the sink before I could protest.

"You cooked," I said, following him. "I'll wash."

"You drew the short straw," he said, rinsing anyway. "I'm bigger, so I win."

"Is that how logic works now?"

He shot me a look over his shoulder, water dripping from his hands. "Worked just fine so far."

I laughed, bumping his hip as I slid in with the dish towel. "Fine, I'll dry."

We moved in rhythm, quiet clinks of dishes filling the kitchen. The kind of simple routine I hadn't realized I'd missed until now. By the time everything was put away, my chest felt lighter, like the air had been scrubbed clean.

"Movie?" he asked, wiping his palms on the towel.

I raised a brow. "You picking?"

"Yeah, 'cause if it's up to you, we'll be sittin' through something with subtitles and violins."

"You don't like foreign films?"

"Not when I can't pronounce nobody's name." He grinned, already heading to the couch.

I shook my head, but the smile tugging at my mouth gave me away. I pulled a blanket from the armrest, dropped beside him, and tucked my legs under me. He scrolled, landed on an old action flick, and hit play.

The room dimmed with the screen's glow, shadows softening across the walls. I curled closer, my shoulder pressed to his chest, the steady thump of his heart under my ear. His arm came around me easily, naturally, pulling me tighter until the world outside the apartment might as well not have existed.

On screen, cars flipped and explosions roared, but all I felt was the slow rise and fall of his breathing.

"You comfy?" he murmured, his lips brushing the top of my head.

"Mm-hmm," I answered, snuggling deeper. "Could get used to this."

"You better," he said, a smile in his voice.

I tilted my chin to look up at him. "You really think you can boss me into comfort?"

He kissed my forehead, slow and certain. "Nah. Just makin' sure you know where you belong."

Silence stretched then, not awkward—just full. I let it wrap around me, let the rhythm of the movie and the warmth of his body ease the last of the tension out of my muscles.

Before long, my eyes grew heavy, lids fluttering against the glow of the TV. I felt his hand rub slow circles into my back, steadying me like an anchor.

When I drifted, half in sleep, half listening, his voice brushed soft against my hair. "Ain't no shadow from your past gettin' through me, Jay. Not while I'm here."

I didn't answer—couldn't. But the way I breathed deeper into his chest said enough.

ten

THE LAST STREAM

THE SUN HAD BARELY STARTED its climb when I rolled outta bed, the soft rustle of sheets behind me the only sound in the house. Jaylah was still asleep, her body curled into the side I'd just left, her curls spread across my pillow. It hit me like it did every morning—I was home. Not just in this house I'd bought, but in the life we'd built since I got out.

It had been weeks since we moved in together. Weeks of waking up with her skin warm beside me, her scent stitched into the air, and the hum of Rooted Words—her dream turned real—just a block away. Every day felt like a blessing I didn't ask for but got anyway. And I didn't take any of it for granted.

I padded down the hallway, barefoot on cool wood floors, and made my way to the kitchen. The smell of coffee still lingered from last night, and I poured what was left into a mug, heating it on the stove while the early light crept in through the windows. Our windows. Our kitchen.

The quiet was different now. It used to feel like a

threat, like something might come crashing through it. But now it felt like peace. Still. Sure.

I checked my phone while the coffee warmed—Malik had already sent the numbers for today's trades. My other life. The one I balanced with this new rhythm. Me and him had built our own corner in the market, flipping stocks with the kind of precision you only learn after years of scraping. But now, I moved smarter. More careful. I had Jaylah to think about.

I was halfway through sipping when I heard soft steps behind me. I turned, and there she was, wrapped in my old T-shirt, bare legs peeking out, eyes still foggy from sleep.

"Didn't mean to wake you," I said, voice low.

She gave a little shrug, walking into me without a word, resting her head on my chest. My arms came up on instinct, wrapping around her like they belonged there—which they did.

"I like waking up to you not gone," she mumbled, voice muffled against my chest.

"You gon' make a man give up his whole career for mornings like this," I murmured, kissing the top of her head.

She laughed softly. "I thought you were the provider, Mr. Stocks and Steady Hands."

I chuckled, holding her tighter. "Still am. Just sayin'—you temptin'."

We stood like that for a while, no rush in either of us. Just quiet. Just the feel of each other.

Eventually, she pulled back, looked up at me with something soft in her eyes. "You make me feel like I'm not on display anymore… like I'm home."

I didn't say nothin' for a second. Just let that settle. She meant it. I felt it in her voice, saw it in the way her body leaned into mine.

"Jaylah," I said, slow and firm. "Ain't nobody gon' ever make you feel like a showpiece again. You hear me?"

She nodded, eyes glossin' just a bit. I kissed her then—slow, sure—like I was sealing a promise.

The morning moved on, and we got ready together like we always did now. She packed a few books in her tote, checked her calendar on her phone, and fussed over her keys. I just watched, leaned against the doorframe, takin' her in like a man who knew how lucky he was.

We walked to the bookstore together, hand in hand. The streets are still quiet, and the shops are just waking up. Rooted Words sat like a jewel on the corner—her name in the window, shelves full of dreams inside.

She unlocked the door and stepped in first, flipping on the lights. Warm amber spilled across the floor, catching on the stacks and displays. Her whole face lit up.

"You still look at this place like it's brand new," I said, watching her.

"It feels that way every time," she replied. "Like I did the impossible."

"You did," I said simply.

We moved around the shop, setting things in place. I wasn't always here with her, but today felt different. I wanted to be. Needed to.

While she organized a display of poetry books, I watched her from behind the counter. That same woman who once hid pieces of herself behind passwords and screens now stood proud in a space she built with her own hands. That kind of growth? That kind of healing? That's sacred.

Jaylah turned, caught me watching. Her smile curved slowly.

"You gon stare all morning or help me lift these boxes?"

I grinned. "Both."

She rolled her eyes, but I saw the way her cheeks warmed. I walked over, kissed her quickly, then grabbed the box.

Life had changed. Not flashy. Not loud. Just real. And standing there with her, in the place she made, I knew something deep in my bones.

We wasn't just surviving anymore.

We was living.

Together.

Late afternoon sun spilled long over the sidewalk, and the air had that soft gold tint to it that said summer still had a few punches left in it. I left the bookstore with Jaylah's kiss still clinging to my cheek, her voice in my ear reminding me to take a damn break. Said I needed it. That I deserved it. And maybe I did. But part of me still hated being away too long.

She was back there now, shelving books, organizing invoices, probably barefoot behind that counter she loved like a second skin. Rooted Words smelled like her now. Felt like her too. Peaceful. Intentional. Built with both our hands. Every corner of it held something sacred.

I took the Charger down the block, windows half down, letting the city air wash through. Malik picked the spot tonight—some quiet bar near the South Loop that had decent wings and cold beer. Said we needed to check in. Not about business. Not even really about life. Just to breathe without women talking circles around us.

When I walked in, Malik was already at the bar, one

boot hooked on the bottom rung, pint in hand. He nodded once, that same calm weight he always carried with him. I slid into the stool beside him, clapped his back.

"You look less like a man dodging parole these days," he said with a smirk.

"That's 'cause I ain't," I replied, flagging the bartender. "Life moves differently now."

"So I see."

We ordered wings, settled into the kind of silence that only came from years of knowing each other—that bone-deep trust that didn't need fluff. The beer was cold, the music just loud enough to blur out other conversations. Malik asked about the house. I told him it felt like a house now. Not just four walls. Not a place I was crashing or passing through.

"So what changed it?" he asked, sucking sauce from his fingers, eyes steady.

"Jaylah," I said, no hesitation. "She put her name on the walls without even tryin'. Everything in there feel like her. Soft, but real. That kinda softness that don't fade."

Malik gave a low grunt, something like agreement. "You look solid, man. Like you been sleepin' through the night."

"Most nights, yeah," I admitted. "Ain't used to it, but I ain't fightin' it either."

We talked a little more. About trades we were watching. About Malik's nephew starting college. About how time moves differently once you realize you don't have to run anymore. I was nursing my second beer when my phone buzzed on the bar.

I glanced at the screen. A link. From Jaylah.

Siren.

My stomach twisted. I stared at the name like it was a mistake, like maybe the letters would shift into something else. But they didn't. Just that clean, bold font and the stream notification. Live.

"You good?" Malik asked, tilting his chin toward my hand.

"Yeah," I said too fast, shoving the phone back in my pocket. My jaw clenched. "Need to step out."

I left half a beer on the bar and didn't say anything more. Outside, the city lights were flicking on, windows glowing in every direction. But all I saw was that damn link. That name.

She hadn't streamed since the night I came home. I told her that was the last time—that she was done. That she didn't need to bare herself to strangers anymore. And I meant that. We both did.

I fished my phone back out, thumb hovering over the link. I didn't want to click it. Didn't want to see her on that screen, not like that. But I had to know.

Still, I didn't tap it. I turned, stalked toward the Charger like I could outrun the burn building in my chest. If this was what it looked like, we were gonna have a problem.

She knew what that site did to me. What it meant. It wasn't just a job, not to me. It was a wound. A reminder of all the nights I couldn't reach her, all the times I had to watch her touch herself for strangers because it paid better than peace.

Traffic moved slowly, like it knew I was trying to get somewhere fast. My hands gripped the wheel tighter every block I crossed. I ran every red I could justify, didn't breathe right until I turned onto our street.

The house glowed warm at the end of the block. Porch light on. Curtains drawn. Like nothing was wrong.

I cut the engine and got out, phone still clenched in my

hand. My feet were too heavy on the porch steps. My breath came fast.

Inside, the living room was dim. Music played low. And there they were—cameras. Set up like they had been months ago. One pointed toward the back hallway. Another near the couch.

I froze, heart hammering.

Then she stepped out. Jaylah. Hair loose. Body wrapped in silk that shimmered like water. Her mouth curved, soft and knowing.

"You came quickly," she said, voice dipped in syrup.

Everything inside me twisted. Then snapped into place.

She wasn't streaming.

She wasn't streaming for them. She'd used the platform to get me home—a message meant only for me.

Jaylah tilted her head, eyes gleaming. "You gonna just stand there? Or you wanna tell me how mad you are?"

I didn't answer. Just locked the door behind me, stalked toward her slowly.

This wasn't about betrayal. It was a test. A reminder. A tease. And I was ready to meet her right where she left the line drawn.

"You really wanna play with me like this?" I finally asked, my voice low.

She gave a small nod, that quiet defiance she wore so well flashing in her eyes. "I wanted your attention."

"You had it," I said, stepping in close, my hands gripping her waist. "But now you got all of me."

In one smooth motion, I scooped her up, her legs wrapping instinctively around my waist. She gasped, hands gripping my shoulders as I carried her across the room. I laid her down in the center of the bed, her silk robe fanning out around her like fire.

"You remember what we said, Jay?" I asked, leaning over her, my voice barely above a growl. "About that camera shit?"

"I remember," she whispered. "I just wanted to remind you what you have."

My lips brushed her ear. "You ain't gotta remind me, baby. I never forgot. But now you're gonna feel it."

Her eyes fluttered shut for half a second, her breath catching again as I trailed my fingers down her body. I slid the robe open slowly, exposing her inch by inch, watching goosebumps rise under my touch. I palmed her breasts, thumbs rolling over her nipples until they peaked under my hands.

She moaned, hips shifting, back arching. I grinned against her neck, loving how easily her body responded to me.

"Hands up," I commanded, and she obeyed, stretching her arms over her head. I reached for the restraints we kept tucked in the nightstand, securing her wrists to the headboard with practiced ease.

"You good?" I asked, my voice soft against her skin.

She nodded. "Yes."

"Color?"

"Green."

I kissed her slowly, savoring the taste of her, the way she melted into it, before I pulled back and grabbed the vibrator from the drawer. Her eyes tracked it, already wide with anticipation.

"You don't get to cum until I say so," I warned, flipping the switch and watching her shudder at the low hum.

I teased her first, letting the toy trace the curve of her inner thigh, avoiding where she wanted it most. Her hips bucked, her breath turning ragged.

"Kairoh," she whined.

"Uh-uh," I said, tapping her thigh. "You wanted to play, baby. Now you wait."

I leaned in, sucking one nipple into my mouth while I pressed the vibrator lightly against her clit. She gasped, her whole body straining against the cuffs. I worked her up slow, driving her to the edge and pulling back just when she started to shake.

She was trembling now, eyes glassy, mouth parted.

"Please," she begged.

"Please what?" I asked, trailing kisses down her stomach.

"I want you. I need to cum."

I smirked. "Not yet."

I grabbed the plug next, slicked it, and eased it into her with careful pressure. Her moan was sharp, her body arching. I kissed the inside of her thigh, sucking a mark into her skin.

"You mine?" I asked, my voice rough.

"All yours," she breathed.

"Say it again."

"I'm yours, Kairoh. Every part of me."

That's all I needed.

I grinned, my eyes locked on hers, seeing the desperation and desire that mirrored my own. "Good girl," I murmured, my hand trailing down her body, teasing her skin with light touches that made her squirm. "You ready for me to take what's mine?"

She nodded, her breath coming in short gasps. "Yes. Please, Kairoh. I need you."

I shifted, positioning myself between her thighs, my body pressing against hers. I could feel her heat, her wetness, and it drove me wild. I leaned down, capturing her mouth in a fierce kiss, my tongue exploring her depths as my hands roamed her body, claiming every inch.

I broke the kiss, my breath ragged. "You're so fucking beautiful like this," I growled, my voice low and rough. "All tied up and ready for me."

She whimpered, her hips lifting, seeking friction. "Good girl, taking me so deep. No one else could handle me like you do."

"Kairoh," she moaned, her voice a plea. "You feel so good."

I gripped her hips, pulling her closer, my body pressing against hers. "Look at you, dripping for me… you're perfect, baby. Fucking perfect."

She gasped, her body arching into mine. "I'm yours, Kairoh. Only yours."

I trailed kisses down her neck, my hands roaming her body, claiming every inch. "That's it—scream for me. You're everything I ever wanted."

She cried out, her nails digging into my back, her body clenching around me. "I scream for you, Kairoh. Always."

I pulled back, my eyes locked on hers, seeing the desire and need reflecting back at me. "I came home for one thing—you. And I'm not leaving this bed until you're ruined for anyone else."

She nodded, her body trembling, her breath coming in short, sharp gasps. "Ruin me, Kairoh. Make me yours."

I grinned, my hands tightening on her hips as I thrust into her, my body moving with a fierce intensity. "You were my best friend, my only weakness, and now you're my dirty little obsession."

She moaned, her body convulsing, her inner muscles clamping down. "Your obsession, Kairoh. Forever."

I increased my pace, my body slamming into hers, the bed creaking under the force of our movements. "You're mine, Jaylah," I growled, my voice low and rough. "All mine."

She nodded, her body trembling, her breath coming in short, sharp gasps. "Yes," she whispered. "Yours. Always yours."

I leaned down, capturing her mouth in a fierce kiss, my tongue exploring her depths as my body continued to move against hers. I could feel her tightening around me, her body on the edge of release.

I broke the kiss, my voice a low growl. "Cum for me, baby. Let me feel you cum all over me."

Her body convulsed, her inner muscles clamping down as she came hard, her cries filling the room. "Kairoh!" she screamed, her voice raw and hoarse.

I rode out her orgasm, my body moving with hers, drawing out every last shudder. As she came down, I slowed my movements, my body still hard and ready. I leaned down, kissing her gently, my touch softening. "You're so fucking perfect," I murmured against her lips. "I love you, mamas."

She smiled, her eyes glistening with unshed tears, her voice soft and breathless. "I love you, too, Kairoh. More than words can say."

I reached up, unbuckling the restraints from her wrists, massaging her skin gently to restore circulation. "How do you feel, baby?" I asked, my voice filled with concern and tenderness.

Jaylah stretched her arms, a contented sigh escaping her lips. "Amazing," she whispered. "So loved and cherished."

I nodded, a soft smile playing on my lips. "That's all I ever want for you," I said, leaning down to capture her mouth in a tender kiss. "To feel loved and cherished, always."

I helped her sit up, my arms supporting her as she

adjusted to the change in position. "Let's get you cleaned up," I murmured, my voice soothing and gentle.

I grabbed a warm, damp cloth from the nightstand, carefully cleaning her body with gentle, loving touches. Jaylah watched me, her eyes filled with adoration and trust. "You take such good care of me," she said, her voice soft and filled with emotion.

"I always will," I replied, my voice firm and resolute. "You're my everything, Jaylah. My heart, my soul, my world."

She reached out, cupping my face in her hands, her thumbs brushing gently against my skin. "And you're mine," she whispered. "Forever and always."

I finished cleaning her, tossing the cloth aside before pulling her into my arms, cradling her close. "Rest, baby," I murmured, my voice a soft lullaby. "I've got you. Always."

Jaylah snuggled closer, her body relaxing against mine, her breath evening out as sleep claimed her. I held her tight, my heart full and content, knowing that in her arms, I had found my home.

As I drifted off to sleep, I knew that no matter what challenges life threw our way, we would face them together. Our love was unbreakable, our bond unshakable. And in that knowledge, I found a peace that I had never known before.

The room was quiet, the only sounds the soft breaths of Jaylah sleeping peacefully in my arms. I pressed a gentle kiss to her forehead, whispering, "I love you, mamas. Forever and always."

And with that, I closed my eyes, ready to face whatever the future held, secure in the knowledge that as long as I had Jaylah by my side, I could handle anything.

The End

C.M. Campbell is a stay-at-home mom, lifelong reader, and storyteller who finally decided to take the leap in 2025. Though she's been writing for years, it wasn't until recently that she gave herself permission to treat it like more than just a dream.

For her, stories have always been a place of healing—a way to find light in the shadows and softness after survival. Through every character and chapter, she writes with purpose: to honor Black love, growth, and legacy. Her books are rooted in real emotion, rich intimacy, and the quiet power of choosing yourself.

When she's not writing, you can find her in the thick of motherhood, curled up with a book, or building the kind of life she used to only imagine.

also by cm campbell

Colliding Into His Arms

In My Rhythm

Beneath His Stetson